Melanie McFadyea...........................*en,*
Britain's bestselling ....ear
of today's teenage g..out
taking risks – and ....ving
up and finding a v...the
wonderful, intense world of ....ries.
Two stories about love: in one, love hidden from parents in
a sleepy Irish seaside town; in the other, love between a
white girl and a black boy, describe dangerous and defiant
relationships that leave all sides – parents too – that bit
wiser. Melanie McFadyean does not shy away from facing
the harsher aspects of being a teenage girl in the 1980s: in
'The Poodles of Doom' she tackles head-on the guilt and
confusion that follows seduction and rape. But she also has
an eye for sheer delight, so here too is a 'bit of romance' on a
Greek holiday, and a funny irreverent bout with the Great
God 'O' Level.
These short stories unerringly capture the humour, chag-
rin and heady exuberance of finding one's way in the world.

Melanie McFadyean was born in 1950 in London. She has
had lots of jobs: waitress, office girl, working on trains
as a market researcher, youth worker, teacher, freelance
journalist and advice columnist. She is co-author of *Only
The Rivers Run Free: Northern Ireland The Women's War*
and *Thatcher's Reign: A Bad Case of the Blues*. A contribu-
tor to many magazines and newspapers, she has written for
*Honey, Company, New Society, The Daily Express, Sun-
day Times* and *City Limits*. She is often invited on to
television and radio programmes to discuss issues affecting
teenagers. For ten years she taught English at Hackney
College of Further Education and, frustrated by the lack of
contemporary fiction for teenage girls, inspired by her
students and the letters she receives at *Just Seventeen*, she
decided to write *Hotel Romantika*.

Virago Upstarts is a new series of books for girls and young women. Upstarts are about love and romance, family and friends, work and school – and about new preoccupations – because in the last two decades the lives and expectations of girls have changed a lot. With fiction of all kinds – humour, mystery, love stories, science fiction, detective, thrillers – and nonfiction, this new series will show the funny, difficult, and exciting real lives and times of teenage girls in the 1980s. Lively, down-to-earth and entertaining, Virago's new list is an important new Upstart on the scene.

Hotel Romantika

and Other Stories

MELANIE McFADYEAN

VIRAGO UPSTARTS

Published by VIRAGO PRESS Limited 1987
41 William IV Street, London WC2N 4DB

Copyright © Melanie McFadyean 1987

British Library Cataloguing in Publication Data

McFadyean, Melanie
  Hotel Romantika and other stories. —
  (Virago upstarts)
  I. Title
  823′.914 [F]   PR6063.A217/

  ISBN 0-86068-918-2

  Typeset by Florencetype Ltd of Kewstoke, Avon
  Printed in Great Britain by Cox & Wyman
  of Reading, Berkshire

Contents

For Jessie and Alice

Acknowledgements

Thank you to the following friends for their help and encouragement: Bert MacIver, Nadine Cartner, Lesley Gwyther, Kim Longinotto, Joanna Rollo, Jeanette Baker, Jacqui Harvey, Cathy Bryant, Neil Middleton, Ciaran Debaroid, Andy Hall.

Thank you also to all the students I have taught who over the years have probably taught me more than I have taught them. Likewise, thank you to all the *Just Seventeen* readers who have written to me, their letters are greatly appreciated.

A very special thank you to Lenore Goodings for her helpful, sensitive editing, her patience and good humour.

The Great God "O" Level

Everyone was sitting in rows waiting for the exam paper to be slipped onto their desks. I didn't actually feel as sick with nerves as I'd expected, which was a nice surprise. It was English 'O' level. Composition. There were about two hundred kids in the hall. I looked at my friends. There was Martin, Miss had been helping him a lot because he said if he didn't get his 'O' level this time his girlfriend said she'd leave him. Miss said nobody was worth it if they made threats like that and Martin was really nice anyway. She's like that, the teacher we had this year. Martin had a thing about homosexuals. He used to say they were disgusting. Miss said they weren't. Martin *always* brought it up in every lesson and Miss kept saying, we are not discussing this topic today, Martin! Finally she had enough. She put her hand on Martin's arm (he really liked Miss) and said, Martin, I'm a lesbian. And Martin went bananas. When Miss's boyfriend came to meet her at the end of the day (he always picked her up), Martin said to him, Excuse me but is it true? And Miss's boyfriend said Yes, because he was joking and anyway he didn't know what Martin was talking about! Martin looked very worried, must be thinking about that girl, what a horrible girl, 'O' levels don't mean you're good or nice or funny.

Keith was a few seats from me. He was wrecked, you could tell by the way his head was bobbing, he was lost

without his Walkman, so he must have been imagining the
music and just having a little dance in his chair. He was
very proud and he was dead cheeky but a really good, nice
person too. The first class ever he strolled in half an hour
late and Miss said, Hello and who are you? He said, Yeah,
cool Miss man, and sat down, his head bobbing. She looked
at him and we all wondered what she'd do. She didn't do
anything, just got on with the lesson, saying things they
always say when they first meet you all about what a
wonderful year you're going to have, promising you videos
and outings if you learn how to use the apostrophe. I
thought she was a bit too relaxed but sort of nice.

Marilyn was three desks away from me looking very
moody, she'd been moody all year. Jaswinder sucked a
sweet, shoving it from one side of her face to the other. She
didn't say anything the first six weeks of term, just whispered yes or no if Miss asked her a question. One thing
I liked about that teacher, she never bullied the quiet ones.
Then Jaswinder said she was so happy because she had
such nice friends for the first time in her life and Miss
looked like she was going to cry, honestly! And three weeks
later this really nice Chinese girl that Jaswinder was friends
with got a job, and poor old Jaswinder cried!

This girl Cindy was pretty and wore high heels and drain-
pipe jeans, she always sat by this little boy called Stevie.
Stevie was like a ten-year-old and I bet he got teased rotten
before he came to our class because he spoke very slowly.
He wrote this essay about his Christmas holidays, it was six
pages long and it gave the title of every tape he'd listened to
and every TV programme he'd seen and everything he'd
had for dinner every day. He only went out twice the whole
holidays. You could tell Miss really liked him. She liked
me too, but at first I thought she showed off too much, tried
too hard to be friends with us. It makes me think there's

something funny about them when they do that. Especially the ones that try and use our slang words and talk about the music we're into. It just sounds funny. Everyone knows they're different to us. I can always tell a teacher by the cars they drive – French ones. It never fails.

There were other kids in the hall that looked like they wanted to put their heads in the oven. All around, by the walls were teachers waiting for someone to cheat. Miss was at the front whispering to one of her friends and pushing the hair out of her eyes. She's always doing that, why doesn't she get it cut, she must be a hippy or something. One thing I like about her is she says she likes singers we've never heard of and she's always amazed we don't know about them. Bob Dylan is one she's always going on about. She even made us read two of his songs, she said they were poetry. I thought they were stupid. One was about some bloke who's on a boat and he goes to a phone box and it says this foot came down the line. It always makes her laugh, she says. The other one was about bad weather but she claimed it was about nuclear war.

Loads of the kids were fidgeting and biting their nails. The PE teacher whose name used to be Pete was there. His eyes were closed. He had changed his name to Ashoka and started wearing orange, and he had these beads with a picture of an Indian man with a beard strung into the beads. He was a really good guy and took us away for weekends. But he was weird! He meditated a lot.

They were coming round slipping a paper face-down onto everyone's desk. Oh no, I thought, what would we have to write about? She said the best thing to do was write about something we knew a lot about. I said, Like what? I don't know a lot about anything. She said, you know a lot about your own life and I said, Who'd want to know about my stupid boring ordinary life, nothing ever happens.

She said, Well something must happen. Yeah, I said, I get up, I go to college, go home, have tea, watch TV, go out on Saturdays. She said, What happened to you when you were a kid, everyone remembers things about being a kid. Yeah, of course, I said, but who'd want to know about that? You'd be amazed, she said. I said, examiners don't want to know what happened to you when you were five, they want to know if you put the apostrophe after the s when there's more than one, and before the s when there's one, and before the s when it ends in something that's not s in the plural. I learned that this year. The only time Miss lost her temper was when even at the end of the Spring term we still couldn't get it right: children's home and girls' tennis rackets. It was always tennis rackets, don't know why, she must have had a thing about them. I said so, and Miss, who wants to know what happened to me after I got potty trained and learned to walk, know what I mean? She said you'd be surprised and everyone laughed because I said yeah, I would. She said, imagine the examiner with this huge enormous pile of exam papers (she always exaggerates) and he/she (she says that sometimes, he/she, in case she offends one or the other, a he or a she) anyway, she said, he/she will like your paper better if you are amusing as well as accurate. Amusing I said, there's nothing amusing about my life. She said she didn't believe me. I unwrapped a piece of gum and started to chew. I was dying for a cigarette. Exams I thought, The great God 'O' level. Just so I can wave a certificate at someone in a suit and tie who's got another 400 where I come from and I'm just number 326. I don't even have a face, I'm a name and a certificate, he, sorry he/she, won't even remember me. I'd just be one of loads of teenagers looking for a job. I probably wouldn't get anywhere anyway because although I've learned the apostrophe, I still can't do punctuation and conversations properly. I imagined this long queue of girls and boys, thousands of us, standing in a line waiting to be rejected or accepted for some job that would probably drive you nuts anyway.

Mr Harding, the head of our course, said, You may start, and everyone turned over their paper. The list of possible essays: 'A Day in the Life of an Old Penny.' I don't believe it! Or, write a story beginning with the words, 'She stepped gingerly from behind a tree . . .' What is gingerly, I wondered, and thought of biscuits and redheads. 'Teenage Unemployment is a thing of the future. How do you see this affecting young people?' Miss said avoid those ones, they're the hardest to do well, she said. Then there was, 'Write a dialogue between a teenager and his/her parents in which they discuss whether or not he/she should be allowed to stay out late at weekends.' I put my head in my hands, God, what a crummy collection of questions. I remembered this smartarsed kid in class, he hardly ever turned up, but he was quite funny sometimes. Once Miss gave us some essay titles because we couldn't think of our own, and this kid says, I'd sooner write about the sex life of a pingpong ball. Miss laughed, but you could see she felt a bit cornered. I read the rest of the questions. The next one was 'Childhood Memories'. I'd already told her I didn't have anything interesting to say about my childhood and my boring, stupid life. I started to chew my biro. I looked round, my mate Valerie smiled at me and rolled her eyes. I must have gone on chewing for a long time because I chewed right through the biro and the ink went into my mouth. I dug out the chewing gum, which was really revolting with all gob and ink on it, and wrapped it as quietly as I could in the chewing gum wrapper hoping nobody would notice. This boy next to me did and he sort of let me know what a slob he thought I was, he made this how

could you be so disgusting face so I gave him a small V sign.
You could tell he was the sickening swotty type and also
very smooth and well dressed. Boys. I've never got on with
them for as long as I can remember, with a very few
exceptions. You can't trust them. I started writing without
really noticing . . .

When I was a kid we lived next door to five brothers.
Their mother always wanted a girl so I used to go and talk
to her. She taught me to peel potatoes and dig out the
eyes. She was tall and shaggy. Her husband was tall and
shaggy too, he was a Communist and everyone in the
street said so but I didn't mind, I liked him. He was kind
and treated me no differently from his boys. The boys
were all older than me but Mick and Chris were only one
and two years older. They used to play these tricks
on me sometimes. The oldest brother, who I didn't know
because he was about eighteen, built a hut in their back
garden. They said I could go in it and I was the only girl
they were letting in. They said they were letting me
because I wasn't like the other girls. I fell for it. They said
I even looked like a boy because I had such short hair and
I wore jeans. I went into the hut, it smelled funny, oily.
There was a hatch in the floor and they said under the
hatch was their secret place and they had supplies there
(they called everything they got their hands on 'supplies',
which was mostly food taken from their parents' kitchen).
They said go on, go down the hatch. I felt proud to be
invited. They said you go first and then we'll come down.
I climbed down. Make yourself comfortable, said Mick, so
I sat on this cushion and then they put down the lid and
bolted it. They left me there for hours. When they came
back to let me out I didn't let them see how much I
minded being locked up like that. I'd been crying. They
let me out, and I said thankyou and tried to make it look

like I was sauntering home happily, but when I got home
I had hysterics.

Another time they bet me I couldn't climb to the top of
this huge tree in their garden. They double dared me and
said whoever got to the top there was a prize. I climbed to
the top and was sitting on a branch trying not to look down
with my legs dangling and one of them had shinned up
behind me and he grabbed my shoes and pulled them off
and shinned down with them so I had to climb down
barefoot. It was cold and I had to take off my socks so I
wouldn't slip. I tried not to cry as I got down the tree. But
I never cried in front of them. I said I had a brother called
William in Australia and he was coming back soon.

In summer we played out very late because it was light.
Mick and Chris had this tent. They said I could get in the
tent. I thought it would be OK so I got into the tent, they
couldn't shut me into it because it didn't have a door, I told
myself. One of them got in with me and said I could try his
sleeping bag if I wanted. I'd never been in a sleeping bag so
I tried it. They were the toughest kids in the street, they
wouldn't have let any other girls in their tent, I was proud.
Mick zipped up the sleeping bag. It felt funny, it was all
wet and I sniffed at it because it smelled. They killed
themselves laughing, they'd pissed in it. I didn't play with
them for a long time after that.

Then one day one of the older ones came up to the fence
and asked me if I'd like to see their new pet. I really liked
pets. Me and my sister had forty white mice. They kept
breeding. So I went over the fence to see this pet which I
thought would be a dog or a cat or even a mouse. Mick and
Chris were there and Mick pulled this snake from inside
his shirt and before I could dodge, he wrapped it round my
neck. I've never screamed that loud since. I screamed so
loud his mother came out and when she saw what he'd

done, she picked up a stick and whacked him. Soon after that
the snake got killed because they lost it. It went under the
staircarpet and got hoovered over and killed. I was glad.

The brothers played another trick on me soon after that.
They said I could come to their bonfire. I stole some food
from their mum's larder. There was a little hole in the
outside wall leading to their back garden from the larder
which a very small person could crawl in and out of and I
was smaller than them. I was crawling out with some bread
pressed against me, which wasn't easy when you're crawling, when their mum caught me and she said, Lucy I'm
surprised at you, this is very disappointing, I shall have to
tell your mother. That did it.

The next day at school I decided to try and get to know a
boy called William. He had lots of scratches on his legs and
knobbly knees. He was skinny and silent. I had watched
him for ages from our side of the playground. We had a
girls' side and a boys' side. I'm sure six year olds don't fall in
love, but it felt like a version of it. I could see all the kids
respected him. I stood by the fence dividing the girls from
the boys. You never knew when a patrolling nun would
walk past and anyway I didn't want him to catch me looking
at him, so I pretended to be busy chipping the black paint
off the railings, but I looked at him from under my eyelids.
He noticed me and looked at me sideways while smacking
the ground with a stick. Then he strolled my way trying
to look as if he wasn't doing that at all. He came up to
the railings and walked past me trailing his stick along the
fence. I loved banging sticks along fences, in fact I could
happily spend my life doing that. Then he spoke to me,
looking the other way. Want some sweets he said? I said
yes. He said, OK then, go under the hedge. I went under
the hedge just inside the girls' playground and waited for
him, crouched behind the greenery. He waited until there

were no nuns and then slipped in beside me. Show me
your bum he said. I was hypnotized, he'd been my imaginary brother, my saviour, my hero and I couldn't say no. He
held out the sweets, candy kisses we called them, toffees
with white swirls in them in see-through wrappers. I tried
to show him my bum but it was difficult. I got all scratched
by the hedge and then just as he had pressed the candy
kisses into my hand and I was struggling to get my knickers
up and my skirt down without dropping the sweets, he
slipped away and this shadow loomed, dark wings, a
demented umbrella, and it hooked me out of the hedge.
A nun. Dirty naughty wicked little girl, she shrieked.
William was strolling away banging his stick along the
railings, one hand in his pocket. The nun dragged me away
through the playground, screaming and kicking, while
everyone watched and I was still trying to pull my skirt
down and I dropped the sweets. She made me go into the
chapel and pray. She said you'll pray until you're truly
sorry for your sins. I knelt in the chapel and tried to pray. I
stared at the altar. I'd never been in a holy place alone
before. I wasn't crying, I wasn't really frightened, I was
bewildered. Then I saw Jesus sitting on the altar in his
white nighty, his hair all lovely and shiny and wavy. He was
swinging his legs and smiling. I smiled back. I wanted to
speak to him but the nun came in. Well, she said, are you
truly sorry for your sins? I said I saw Jesus, and the nun
grew very angry and called for someone to fetch the
Mother Superior. I was very frightened of the Mother
Superior who although we never saw the nuns' hair, must
have had red hair because she had these bright orange
eyebrows. She swished quietly into the chapel a few minutes later. I shrank. I always got the words superior and
severe muddled up because she was so severe that there
were dents in her lower lip where her sticking out teeth

were permanently sunk into it in anger. She looked down at me and said You'll pray for another fifteen minutes for forgiveness and your mother will be sent for. My mother came and she was taken into the Mother Superior's room. I had to sit outside with the other nun while they were talking. I was very very sad. Then Mother Superior called for me to be brought in and I stood in the middle of the room. She said are you going to apologize now and I looked at my mother. My mother was very very angry and she lost her temper with the Mother Superior, she said to her in this very deep low voice, my child has nothing to apologize for. The Mother Superior said the child needs treatment. She was really furious, you could tell, and my mother got up and took my hand. She said it's perfectly natural for children to behave like that, goodbye, and we left. My mother was very kind and I never had to go back to that school . . .

Time is up, someone was saying. I was still writing and someone said Lucy, stop writing and shush. I was muttering as I wrote. Then the teacher took away the piece of paper I was writing on. Time's up, she said. I crashed back into reality and the present like a rocket re-entering orbit and there was the chewing gum and inkstains and chewed-up biro and the stuck-up boy next to me carefully putting his pens away side by side in his jacket pocket. And I realized I hadn't put in any of the conversations properly with punctuation marks.

First Love ◀

Not a lot happens in my town. It's pretty much like any other Irish seaside town. In summer trippers come with picnic baskets and buckets and spades. When it's sunny they pile onto the beach. The parents get red noses and violent stripes around the limits of their swim suits and everyone is noisy and happy. They eat fish and chips and in the evenings, the teenagers go to one of the discos. There are two. One closes as soon as the season is over and the other stays open but only on Saturday nights. My father won't let me go. He says it's not good to go there because of boys.

I was about to ask again when my mother interrupted my look. She must have guessed what was coming.

'Nuala, go and get the messages and be back in time for your tea,' she said.

'Can I go to the disco tonight?' My mother looks at my father and he looks at his newspaper.

'What do you think, Frank?' she says cautiously.

'Gymslip Teenies in Black Market Disco Pill Racket,' he reads from the *Sun*. I look at my ma. She'd let me go if it wasn't for him. He goes on reading and I stand by the door with two plastic carrier bags for the errands, waiting to see what he will say next. He stares at the newspaper. Anyone would think he was going to find an answer there. Sure enough, he does.

'This is why you're not going to any disco,' he says, shaking the paper and folding it so that only the headline about the Gymslip Teenies shows. 'No daughter of mine is going to end up like that!' he thunders, waving the paper at me. 'Read it! Go on read it for yourself!' I back off, twisting the plastic bags in my hands.

'Well, if you won't read it for yourself, I'll read it to you. "Gymslip Teenie Tracey Donaldson, fifteen, counts the cost of her under-aged affair with Disco Romeo, Steve Jones . . ."' he droned on. It was about girls somewhere in London who couldn't get the Pill because the law had changed. 'And a damn good thing too,' said my father. The doctors wouldn't give it to the girl without her parents' consent. Her father refused permission. She went to the disco and she and her friends bought packets of the Pill from older girls. They had shoplifted and sold things to pay for the Pill – £15 a packet on the black market. My father paused in his reading and looked at me with hard eyes. 'And that is the sort of thing that goes on in discos. No girl of mine is taking the Pill, do you hear?'

My brother Kevin stamped across the room and turned up the volume on the TV. My father said nothing about that, just 'And that's final!' Then he joined Kevin in cheering on their team with 'That's it, wee lad!' and, 'Kick the bastard' and, 'Foul! Ref!'

I twiddled the bags between my fingers until they were nearly in bits. I thought of the disco. I really wanted to go. What else was there in this town? Family life, rows and recriminations, chores, housework, homework, school, chapel, breakfast, TV, dinner and tea. Year in, year out. But there was life at the disco.

My ma sighs as she darns, she's always doing something or other, sewing, washing, ironing. I help her, and so do my sisters. The boys don't. Patrick comes in. He treads mud into the carpet. He joins Kevin and my father. I pluck up courage to ask again.

'Well?' I say. I have to shout above the noise of the TV. He reads on. He's back to the *Sun*, through the news bit and trying to make out he's not looking at the page three *Sun* Bird. That embarrasses me and my mother. She always pretends he's not really looking at the bosoms spilling out over the page. She once said something and he shouted at her and said there was nothing wrong with it. She couldn't explain why she didn't like it. He said she had no sense of humour and went on looking at the girl. I went into the kitchen to help her. She was sitting at the table, her head in her arms. She was crying quietly. All she said was, 'Don't tell him, you're too young to understand' as she dabbed at her eyes with her handkerchief. I wanted to help her but I didn't know what to say. I put my hand on her shoulder. She controlled herself and gave me a hug. 'Off you go, don't be long.'

I wished I had the nerve to tell my father what I thought of him. I could have begun by telling him that in our town you couldn't even get the Pill if you were a grown woman because the doctor didn't approve of it and the chemist didn't even stock condoms. There certainly wasn't any black market! Besides, I didn't want the Pill. I just wanted to go to the disco.

I went out to do the errands. As I walked along the street I met Siobhan.

'You coming tonight?' she said. I was embarrassed and miserable and I didn't say anything.

'Your dad?' she asked. I nodded.

'Why is he so mean?'

'He says I'll take the pill.' I saw him in my mind looking

at the Sun Bird's bosoms and I burst into tears. Siobhan
took my arm and steered me along the street to a café.

'Two teas,' she said. 'Here, drink this and stop crying.'
She pushed a cup towards me.

'I wish I could go,' I said through my blocked nose.

'We'll think of something,' Siobhan said narrowing her
eyes and smiling. 'We'll think of something.'

'Even if I could I wouldn't have anything to wear,' I said.
'And I've no money. Do you know, once I asked him for
some money for this dress I saw in a shop. "Do you think I
work all week at the farm so you can buy dresses?" he said.
My married sister Ann was there and she said under her
breath, "Nuala never gets a thing, mean old bastard." He
thumped her even though she's twenty-one. She hasn't
been home since. My ma said, "Your father does his best",
but she was kind of wringing her hands, trying to keep
the peace.'

'We'll think of something for another Saturday,' Siobhan
said getting out her pocket mirror and checking her mascara because Sean Brown had come in with one of his
mates. I shrank.

'Coming down the disco tonight?' he said to her boldly,
chewing some gum.

'Might be,' she replied.

'See you there then,' he said and swaggered off to the
pinball machine. We got up to go and I admired the way
Siobhan walked in her mini-skirt and high heels which
went click click. I was wearing trainers and jeans and
looked younger than fifteen. She looked older, a bit like
Tracey Donaldson, the girl in the Teenie Pill picture, who
was gorgeous. Siobhan's got fashionable short hair all spiky
and sometimes she puts gel in it to make it stick up. Other
times she oils it down, she copies pictures in girls' magazines. She's got really nice grey eyes and she's tall. I could

tell she really fancied Sean by the way she ignored him so much he had to notice. She took my arm and I shuffled out beside her but I banged into the door as we left. Sean Brown laughed and I glanced over my shoulder. I noticed that his mate wasn't laughing, he was looking at me sort of seriously and my heart jumped.

That Saturday night dragged and dragged. My father went to the pub and Kevin went off with his mates; nobody even asked him where he was going but then he is a boy. I ate my tea and washed up. I put my little sisters to bed and watched TV with my ma. The copy of the *Sun* my father had used against me was left folded so the headline jumped out at me. I read a bit of the article he hadn't mentioned anything about. It said that the boys wouldn't go and buy sheaths because they were embarrassed and so they were using clingfilm. In England the kids can go and buy sheaths in the chemist. I didn't want my ma to know I'd been reading it and I felt embarrassed. Clingfilm!

Later I lay on my bed and listened to my favourite tapes: songs about boys and girls and romance. None of it mine. I looked at the pictures on my wall. Pop stars, ponies, ballerinas. The postcard of the Empire State Building that my oldest and favourite brother sent me. I felt I had nothing. I cried myself to sleep, not for the first time.

Sunday. Breakfast. My father ate eggs and bacon and toast and drank his tea noisily, every Sunday the same routine. After she'd cleared up, my mother said, 'Who's coming to mass, then?' My father always says he has to help someone or other with his car or build something or do overtime. She'd look at me and tell me to get ready. I never dared say no. It was peaceful in the chapel anyway, even my little sisters kept quiet. I looked up at the Virgin with her sad face and then along the rows until I saw Siobhan and her ma. Siobhan winked. Every week the sermon was the same, hell and damnation and the wicked. The 'decline of civilization' was a phrase that he used every single time. I didn't listen.

After mass, I walked along the seafront with Siobhan. Our mothers walked along behind, their conversation full of 'he' did this and 'he' said that and 'they're all the same,' and 'God forgive me'. Siobhan had a love bite on her neck.

'How'd you get that?' I asked her, impressed.

'Sean,' she said laughing proudly. 'He's gorgeous, I swear. He says he loves me!'

I listened, fascinated. I'd never been near a boy. 'And he says his mate really fancies you.' The boy in the cafe!

'He asked Sean to ask me to ask you if you'd go out with him. So I'm asking.'

'What's his name?'

'Gerry MacFarlane.'

'Who'd he dance with?'

'Nobody, he played the fruit machine and space invaders and stuck with his mates.'

'Where's he from, anyway?'

'I don't know, I haven't seen him around until recently. Is the interrogation over? Do you want to go out with him or what?'

'Dunno.' Of course I did, I was dying to say yes.

'Sean says he's very shy and doesn't usually go with girls but he likes you.'

'He's never even met me!'

'Well, he likes you anyway. What'll I tell Sean to tell him? Will you or won't you?'

I knew my father would never let me. I told Siobhan that and she said, 'Oh, for God's sake, you can't go on doing everything according to your father forever. My father says if I'm in by twelve it's OK. Why can't yours?'

'I told you, he says if you go to discos you'll take the Pill.'

'Some chance in this town! Anyway it's better than getting pregnant like poor Maureen.'

'Sssssh! My ma'll hear you!'

'Well, do you want to go out with him or not?!' said Siobhan.

'Yes, but my fa . . .'

'Oh never mind your father, you'll just have to tell him a lie.'

The week was like any other week. Mother Theresa gave us a lecture wearing her very special pained expression. 'If you frequent the dance halls and vice halls you will be soiled and spoiled. Every girl must protect her precious flower in observance of her holy duty, with regard for the Holy Virgin Mary . . .' Siobhan yawned openly. I wished I had her nerve. Everyone giggled. Mother Theresa's face cracked like lightning. 'Siobhan Murphy, you will stay behind!'

Siobhan stood in the middle of a group of excited girls in the playground.

'1986!' she began. She was going to make one of her speeches. 'There's computers and aeroplanes going faster and further and contraception and digital watches and the nuns tell you to bless the Virgin!' We loved her nerve, she outraged and delighted us. As she held forth she whipped out her pocket mirror and artfully smoothed bright red glossy lipstick on her mouth. She contined: 'They'll be taking us in a bus to see a moving statue of our lady next like all the other suckers. They'll never make me believe she had a baby without doing you know what!' She walked back into class after improving briefly on her lipstick.

Mother Theresa's voice boomed, 'Wipe that muck from your mouth!' Siobhan didn't move a muscle. She would be kept in every day, sent to pray in the chapel and a letter would be sent to her parents. Siobhan didn't care.

'London,' she'd say whenever she got into trouble. 'I'll go to London and have a flat of my own and I won't get married and I'll take the Pill if I want to, I'll have a job and my own life and go to clubs.' We believed her, we envied her, we took pride in her, we expected her to make us free, if anyone could it was her.

I waited for her on Friday for the hour of her detention after school. She'd thought up a plan which she told me about as we walked along arm in arm. 'Tell them I'm babysitting because my ma's going to see my granny and my father's going out. We'll be back before him and if they ask, he can say you were with me. I'll bribe Patrick and Steven. They owe me favours anyway and if they won't do it, I'll threaten them. I know a thing or two about them and where they go! They'll be babysitting and we'll be out dancing!' She had it all planned.

'But is your ma really going to see your Gran?'

'Yes, but not until Sunday, but your parents'll never know.'

Siobhan lived at the other end of the town and her parents and mine didn't get on very well. My parents thought hers let Siobhan get away with too much. Siobhan and I laughed with excitement. I'd never told a major lie before although I knew that my father lied to us. Some lies, I thought, were a betrayal, some cowardice, some cheating. But there were others that were to do with justice. I was taking what was mine – a little bit of independence. Siobhan helped me see it that way.

'Da,' I said at teatime that evening. He munched on, heaving huge forkfuls into his mouth and making horrible noises like a mechanical digger. My ma had this tight line around her mouth and her nostrils would flare, and I wondered how she could love him. He slopped his tea in his saucer and his big hairy hands were filthy.

'What?' he said, not bothering to glance up from his overloaded plate.

'Siobhan says can I go over to her house tomorrow night as she's babysitting because her ma's away to her Granny's.'

I was amazed how easy it was to tell a lie. I'd rehearsed it so many times that when it came to telling it I could see Siobhan's ma and her grandma sipping tea together by the fire and talking as all the older women did. The conversation full of 'he', lots of weary sighs and phrases explaining life away. 'These things are sent to try us, Maureen' and, 'It's the will of God, surely' and 'Beggars can't be choosers,' and, 'It's the way of the world.' The whole adult female world of a small Irish seaside town worn away like the steps of the chapel by centuries of weariness. There was even something comforting in the repetition, a kind of litany. The devil you knew.

'That Siobhan's a wee slut,' said my father, 'Those mini skirts and high heels and giving the boys the eye.' I bit back the words I'd like to have said. At least, I thought, Siobhan didn't show her breasts in a newspaper so that hypocritical old gits like him could slurp all over them pretending they weren't, while their wives sat by all worn-out with life darning socks and heaving long sighs. I wondered if I'd ever have the courage to answer him back. But this time he'd insulted my best friend and something in me snapped. I knew that the time would come when I'd tell him what I thought of him. I wondered if that's what it meant when it said, 'And the meek shall inherit the Earth'. It was always my favourite bit of the Bible.

'Well, can I babysit or not?' I asked, as calmly as I could.

'Oh Frank, let her go,' my mother said and he grunted, 'OK'. It was as easy as that.

I had to make it look normal when I left for Siobhan's on

the Saturday evening. I carefully hid my mascara, a present from my sister, and folded my tights so I could fit them in my pocket. I never carry a bag, so if I'd suddenly started they might have been suspicious. I wore my miniskirt and a short-sleeved tee shirt under my old dress and dufflecoat. It was a bit bulky and uncomfortable but I'd seen a girl doing this on a TV play when she was running away from home. My ma said, 'Have a nice time,' and I went. I hurried along the street and onto the seafront along to Siobhan's end of the town. I say 'town', but it only took fifteen minutes walking to get from one side to the other. I was scared going past my father's pub. It was a warm spring night and I could hear men's voices and the clink of glasses. I sped past the door and nobody saw me. Two old men sat by the open door reciting memories of their old glory. A ballad drifted out into the night, a wistful lament.

I banged on Siobhan's door full of the thrill of escape and high on the success of my subterfuge, banishing all guilt in my excitement. She grabbed me by the collar and dragged me up to the bathroom and locked the door.

'I didn't want them to see you, they'd think, "Why hasn't she got her disco gear on? And why is she wearing a dufflecoat in the warmest spring night in history?"'

She looked me up and down anxiously. 'You can't go in that old gear!' I took off the coat and peeled off the dress, giggling as the new me appeared. She did a stripper mime. She had loads of make-up on and looked great. She smeared and dabbed and smoothed lots onto my face until I looked at least seventeen. I couldn't stop staring in the mirror.

'You look great!' she said. Then she put some of her red lipstick on me. 'Oh but Jesus, those shoes, you can't go in them!' I'd forgotten, I still had my trainers on. I didn't have any other shoes. She pulled a face. I felt like the old shy

Nuala again, and sat on the edge of the bath fiddling with my fingers and looking at the floor.

She disappeared and came back with a pair of black high heels, sort of fifties. I practised walking in them, it wasn't easy but it had to be worth the trouble. On the way to the disco I stumbled a hundred times. She went ahead of me and as we went past the park she demonstrated how to walk in them. 'Like this,' she said. She swayed and teetered and I tried to copy her. By the time we got there, I almost had the hang of it. There was a thin moon rising and the thumping of the base rhythm of rock and roll music came from the disco. I'd never felt like I did then, a sort of rise of nerve and thrill of fear all mixed up with feeling free and light and like a woman.

It was still quite early, Siobhan explained. In the disco, lights swerved around the empty dance floor, red, blue and yellow. The girls all piled into the ladies, crowding round the mirrors, checking details and taking sidelong glances at each other. Siobhan propelled me out to the bar where Sean was leaning casually. Beside him stood Gerry, who looked uncomfortable. He reminded me of a kid in his Sunday best. Sean introduced me and Gerry, and for a while I wished I'd never come. I hadn't thought about what we'd say to each other. Siobhan and Sean went to dance soon after, leaving us standing there, shoved and jostled by people trying to get a drink. 'Like a drink?' he said very loudly, shouting over the music. I nodded. He got me a coke and I felt silly being only fifteen and drinking soft drinks. It was impossible to talk. Anyway since neither of us knew what to say, it was just as well there was such loud music and so many people. 'Dance?' he shouted. I was very nervous, so I watched Siobhan and tried to copy her and didn't look at Gerry. The shoes made it hard to move and I wished I'd had more practice. Gerry tried to talk to me a couple of times and we knocked into one another. I was beginning to feel disappointed but I so much wanted to like being at the disco. Siobhan came to the rescue, indicating that there was a table at the back where it was quieter.

But still nobody quite knew what to say. Siobhan tried her best. Sean was drinking fast and so was Siobhan. A slow number came on and Siobhan and Sean got into a clinch. Then Gerry asked me to dance and I was embarrassed and then he put his arms round me and it was nice. I was surprised how easy it was, easier than trying to dance any other way in high heels, easier than trying to talk. I got lost in the music, I was happy, I forgot everything. It was as if all the anxiety of home was washed away. I was happier than I've ever been. When Gerry asked me if I'd like to go outside, it felt safe. He led me by the hand. We sat on a step in the cool night and held hands. There was the thin moon, the stars, the sound of the sea. I wondered, was this the same dowdy little town I'd lived in all my life?

'You're not like other girls, not like Siobhan,' Gerry said.

'She's not like other girls,' I said. 'She's my best friend.'

'But you're not like her at all.'

'You mean I'm not bold like her,' I said. I looked at the shoes she'd lent me as if they had carried me into the adult world and she'd made it possible.

'My father and mother think me and Siobhan are baby-sitting, you know.'

'You had to lie to them, did you?'

'Yes, I'm not allowed to go to the disco.'

'Why?'

'My father thinks I'll . . .' I wondered if I should say, he might think I was fast and we were getting on so well. I didn't want to spoil it.

'Thinks what?' he said.

'Thinks I'll take the Pill.' I looked at my feet again

wondering what he'd say and if I'd put him off.

He started to laugh and then I did too and I thought how reckless happiness makes you feel, and I had never felt like that before.

'Will you?' said Gerry putting his arm round me. And then I didn't know what to say and then he kissed me. I'd never been kissed before and I had often thought I wouldn't know how to do it, but it was great. It was really easy. We kissed for ages and then Gerry said he'd walk me home.

'I'll take you home, we can walk along the seafront.' I'd always heard that boys are only after one thing. They said if you didn't they'd leave you and if you did they'd call you a slag anyway. I didn't want to be caught in that trap. I thought of the way women talked about the men. But I trusted Gerry. When I looked at him I felt happy. It must be all right, I thought. My ordinary clothes were in the cloakroom. I fingered the raffle ticket that showed which bag was mine. I would have to tell him I had to put my old dress and my duffle coat on, and my trainers. I panicked, he'd think I was still a kid. But there was no getting out of it and if I didn't change, I wouldn't be able to have him walk me home.

'I have to go and get my clothes and put them over this lot and clean my face completely,' I said wondering if that would be the end of my happiness. He smiled.

'Go on then, I'll wait.'

How did he understand so much? He wasn't like other boys. As I went back in I passed Siobhan and Sean. They were wrapped round each other behind a hedge. I tiptoed past on the crunching gravel and I heard Siobhan suppress a laugh. I got my things and went back to Gerry. He was sitting on the steps and I looked at him as I approached. He had an ordinary face, was an ordinary height and size.

But once I got close up I looked at his eyes, and they were different to other boys'. They weren't greedy. They were hazel, not green, not brown and there was something I couldn't define in them. Was it that he was wiser than most boys of seventeen? Was he sad in some way? I couldn't decide so I put off thinking about it. I felt so much at ease with him, as I would with a best friend, but when he kissed me, the world stopped, time stood still. I put my old clothes on over my miniskirt and tee shirt and sat down to take off the high-heeled shoes. I couldn't take them home with me.

'What'll I do with Siobhan's shoes?' I said, worried.

'Here,' he took them and shoved them into his pockets, grinning. I got out a tissue and started wiping off the remains of the make-up.

'You're not seventeen, are you?' he said as I wiped it all off.

'No,' I said, thinking now he really would back out.

'How old are you?'

'Nearly sixteen,' I said, a little bit desperately.

'I don't care, anyway,' he said and put his arm round me. We walked home along the windy seafront and every so often he'd stop and turn me round to face him and then kiss me.

I made it home by 11.30 and nobody seemed to notice that I was a different person.

'Nuala!' my father shouted. 'Make me a cup of tea and a sandwich.'

No problem, Dad, I thought, and put them in front of him in record time. I even smiled at him. That seemed to shock him, but he just grunted and wrapped his mouth round a sandwich. I wanted to be alone to think about Gerry. I went up to my room and looked in the mirror expecting to see some change in my face. But my face was the same, my mouth was the same despite the kissing, everything was the same except for a brightness in my eyes. I was the same but I'd never be the same again. I was happy. I was scared. I didn't want to tell anyone. I didn't understand. I couldn't sleep and then in the morning I couldn't wake. Life would never be how it used to be. Suddenly I had a secret, something of my own which as long as I kept it hidden couldn't get poisoned or blighted by my father. I knew something he didn't. I found that lying came naturally to me, because it wasn't lying as I had always understood it, it was taking what was mine – my liberty.

I changed. A new boldness came to me. I stopped feeling so shy and awkward. I spoke more, I answered questions in class. I walked with a sure stride. The miracle was the lie. It meant I had told this tyrant, my father, that I'd had enough, and I'd achieved this without any upheaval. Even when I went to confession, I didn't feel I had to confess any lies. I went less and less and nobody tried to force me.

Somehow, Gerry and I managed to meet every weekend for the rest of the spring and summer. The trippers came and went. We took the bus out into the countryside, we walked along hidden paths to secluded smuggler's coves. We told each other everything and we kissed and kissed and kissed.

'Has he asked you for it yet?' said Siobhan one day as we walked to her house after school. I knew what she meant. I didn't know what to say. Suddenly I felt more like my old shy self and she was the wise girl, almost a woman. He hadn't asked for 'it'. The way she said it reminded me of mucky stories in newspapers. It wasn't like that with me and Gerry.

'No,' I said.

'Well, here's your birthday present – it's next week isn't it?'

I nodded. She handed me something in a brown paper bag. I peered into it. Sheaths.

'Where'd you get those? You're not married and you and Sean are under eighteen! Where'd you get them?'

'Oh ways and means.'

'Isn't it illegal?' I said, peering closer into the bag and looking at the instructions, which embarrassed me.

'Look, if it weren't for ways and means of getting those there'd be a population explosion in this town, not just one Maureen O'Dowd but a whole town full of them, and the wrath of God and all of that!'

The great dread was to fall, to get caught as Maureen O'Dowd had. Pregnant at 14 and everyone seeing her belly as it swelled. The nuns wouldn't have her at school. They said she was a bad influence on the younger girls. You'd see her pushing a pram, her mother grim faced beside her, and you'd see her red-eyed after confession as she hurried away from the chapel. Nobody spoke to her, but everybody spoke about her. This she knew. Only me and Siobhan talked to her. One day I met her as she came out of the chapel. She'd obviously been crying.

'Hello, Maureen, how are you?' I asked, falling into step beside her.

'Right enough,' she said miserably.

'Come for a cup of tea?' To my surprise, she nodded.

Maureen's family were good-living, God-fearing and as old-fashioned as time. The eldest son Martin was training for the priesthood and Maureen's mother was always saying, 'It would do nobody in this house a bit of harm to follow Martin's example.' It had been her plan for Maureen to be a nun.

Maureen had the angry disappointed expression of an

ageing woman in the face of a sixteen-year-old girl. I asked her how things were at home.

'Awful,' she said bleakly. 'They don't speak to me except to tell me bad things and call me all the names. My father calls me whore and says I've brought disgrace on the family. "A daughter of mine!" he shouts, and then shakes his head. My mother cries and makes me feel guilty, and if it wasn't for my sister Agnes I don't know how I'd cope. They suffer the child but nobody but me and Agnes shows him any love.' She began to cry.

'But what about the father, Maureen?' I asked. She had never told anyone who the father was.

'Oh them . . .' she said and looked at me in fear.

'Them?' I said, shocked but trying not to show it. 'What do you mean?'

'Oh Nuala, I never told anybody, honest I never. But everyone at home except for Agnes has always been so hard on me and I had sex with two boys. One said he never, you know, well, never actually . . .'

'I know what you mean,' I said.

'And the other had a sheath but it came off just at the last minute. Oh Nuala, I shouldn't have told you, but you won't tell anyone will you?'

'Course not, but what about the boys? Can't you find out which one it is? Surely *they* know it might be them?'

'Oh never mind,' she said wearily, without any bitterness. 'It's best forgotten now.'

Everyone knew she wouldn't tell anyone who the father might be, and I was the only person in the town who knew it could be one of two boys. But I didn't know who they were. I wonder if she even told the priest that. I wouldn't have told him if I were her. He might have spoken to her father, you never knew with that priest, he was sly. Poor Maureen. My mother said it was a tragedy and my father

said, 'Serves her right,' but before he launched into a full
scale speech, I slipped out of the room.

One afternoon Gerry and me were lying under some trees
in the woods hidden from everyone and anyone. Gerry did
something he'd never done before, he undid the buttons of
my blouse. He said, 'Perhaps it's time.' With Gerry,
everything was natural and happened when it should. But
as his hands gently touched bits of me nobody had ever
touched, I thought of Maureen.

'I can't,' I said.

'Why? Don't you think it's right for us the way we are
together?' he said.

'It's not that . . .' It was difficult to explain.

'What then?'

'I saw Maureen yesterday and I can't stop thinking about
her.'

I could see Maureen's beaten expression, I could see her
baby, unloved by her family, prayed for but neglected by
his grandparents. I saw two shadowy silhouettes of boys
with no faces. Gerry said nothing. He went on saying
nothing. I took his silence for the same kind of bewilder-
ment I felt.

'Do you understand?' I said.

He didn't reply. He looked troubled. I thought I must
have hurt him, that he felt that I had rejected him. It was as
though a stone had been cast onto the smooth waters of our
relationship. Something in me flared, something I immediately extinguished.

The evenings got chilly and the trippers had gone. Still
my father showed no signs of suspicion. I had amassed a
network of alibis, had become as skilful as any double
agent. I think my ma knew though. I think she deliberately
said nothing. I sensed a new warmth from her and I

wondered if my love affair reminded her of some unful-
filled fantasy from her past. She helped me with her
absence of questions. Tacitly she collaborated with me
against my father. At home nothing changed, but I was
completely different. I suppose looking back on it, the idyll
had to end. At the time I didn't let myself think about it.

It was tea time and my father was talkative. He had
chosen a subject dear to his prejudices, the misfortune of a
young girl and her downfall in the eyes of all Catholic
fathers such as himself.

'Have you heard about young Maureen O'Dowd's
father? There was a carrying on, I can tell you, swore
vengeance, said he'd had his suspicions all along and that a
little birdy had told him a thing or two. Paternity suits, he
said and a fancy Dublin lawyer, every penny of his savings
to get the little bastard to marry his daughter. You make
your bed and you lie on it, I say.' I shivered as he droned
on. 'Of course it was the stupid wee bitch's own fault, led
him on I've no doubt.' This was a theme he loved.

I slipped away again, saying I was going to Siobhan's,
just as they were settling down to an evening in front of
the TV.

I walked along the seafront, looking at the horizon – the
far limits of our world, further than most of us went in a
lifetime, stuck as we were in this little town, set in its ways.
We were slaves to rules made before time began, as far as I
could see. Siobhan's present was in my pocket. I curled my
fingers around it. I wondered. I heard my father's voice
. . .'ruined future . . . shame on the family . . . wee
slut got what was coming to her . . .' I walked on. By the
time I met Gerry the sun had set black and red. There was
a tenderness in him that night, something different,
an intensity in his look, an urgency in his touch. And
then it seemed the moment, the natural time to make

love. He said, 'My mother and father are away, come to my house.'

I didn't hesitate. He tried no trick to woo me, made no speeches, promised nothing he wouldn't keep to, said very little, murmured, whispered, caressed. In the playground and the toilets the girls had talked about sex. From what I learned, it seemed to be mostly rushed, messy, painful and more often than not disappointing. I'd heard it all. I'd seen Maureen. I knew what it did to girls. What happened with Gerry wasn't like any of the stories I'd heard. It was quiet, intense, strange, wonderful. I didn't tell anyone, not even Siobhan. I carried it like a secret treasure locked in my mind.

After that first time, Gerry and I made love whenever we could. There was always somewhere, a wood or a barn, haystacks left from summer, and we didn't think about the winter. One night in October, as an end-of-summer coldness grew with each day, my mother called me into the kitchen. She beckoned and inclined her head as if to say she had something to tell me. This was unusual.

'Nuala, I know. I know. But don't worry, I won't tell your father. I've watched you these last months and you're a changed girl, a young woman.' She sighed. 'I was too, I remember it.' And then she stopped. There was something she seemed to want to say. She fidgeted. 'As you know it's impossible for an unmarried girl of your age to get contraception. In this town they'd sooner prescribe arsenic.' She stopped, surprised at herself.

'It's all right Ma, I've got, well, we, it's . . . it's OK, Ma, don't worry.' I couldn't bring myself to say the word 'sheath' to my mother. It was like swearing in chapel.

'Well, don't go letting one split on you,' she said. And that was where the conversation ended, one of those conversations in which so much is left unsaid. She got on with her neverending chores.

As the days got shorter and colder, I began to feel different. I thought perhaps it was a mood that came with the end of summer. But as Gerry and me grew closer and closer, I felt strange – as though we were magnetized and that then gravity interfered and cast me off at a tangent, as though I could see his lips move but couldn't understand the words. Whatever this sensation meant eluded me. What was it? It wasn't a question I liked to ask myself because I didn't know what it was I didn't know, so how could I ask? Like an itch in the mind, it was a feeling of being ill at ease that crept up on me at strange times, leaving me defenceless. One night I felt this peculiar mood pervade me more than ever. Something I couldn't name was making a chasm between Gerry and me, something I couldn't reason with, couldn't get the measure of.

I arrived home at the usual time. My father was in one of his unpleasant talkative moods. I could hear his voice battering on as I went into the narrow front hall. I was going to creep up the stairs but he heard me.

'Nuala!!' Reluctantly I pushed open the living room door. He was sitting in his usual chair with the greasy patch where his head rested. My mother sat in her usual chair mending a shirt.

'Well, Nuala, it seems that in spite of her behaviour, young Siobhan Murphy is keeping you out of trouble.' What was he about to say this time, I wondered. Why had he specially called me into the living room? It certainly wasn't like him to say anything good about Siobhan. I stood by the door. My mother didn't look up and smile as she normally did, she seemed to be making an extra effort to concentrate on her sewing. My father looked at me. He was about to start again.

'Some wee girls, on the other hand, are getting what they deserve.'

He went on looking at me. I said nothing.

'Your little friend is really in trouble now.' Meaningful pause. 'It seems Maureen O'Dowd's father has dragged the truth out of the wee bitch, seems he knows who the father is.'

His tone disgusted me. But that was nothing new. I had got used to restraining myself when he started like this.

'I heard he beat the name of the young fella out of her, strapped her.' He looked satisfied. 'Wee bitch,' he said again, and then he chuckled, not a familiar sound coming from him, a mirthless, gravelly, nasty sound. But he had pushed me too far, my restraint wasn't going to hold forever.

'She's not a wee bitch!' I said. His eyes popped in amazement. Nobody ever answered him back. 'She's just a young girl like me or Siobhan or any of us.' It was as if time stood still. My mother paused in her stitching as though a spell had been cast. She had gone pale. In twenty-five years of marriage she'd never dared answer him back. I was shaking with fear but also with excitement. I'd stood up to him. He glared at me in astonished fury.

'Then,' he thundered, 'it'll be of no interest to you to know the name of the young lad her father thinks is responsible will it?'

I wanted to say no, it will be of no interest to me at all, but something prevented me, some deep fear. My mother was looking at him, her eyes pleading, her mouth moving as though she wanted to say something but either didn't dare or couldn't find the words.

'Well,' he started again, still raging and shouting, 'since it may not be of any interest to you, I will tell your mother, who seems to have gone as white as a sheet. I'll tell you who will be walking up the aisle with his new but used bride – young Gerry MacFarlane. His father will horsewhip the young bastard.' His voice seemed to go on forever, 'Whip them into line . . . spoiled and corrupted . . . what can you expect . . .'

I sat down, hearing each word crystal clear, taking in nothing. I was looking straight at him but through him. Eventually he stopped and returned to his newspaper. I got up and left the room without saying anything. I seemed to have gone numb. I went into my bedroom and sat very still on the edge of the bed. Then the crying began. My mother came in quietly and sat beside me. She held me as I wept, held me close as she must have done when I was very young.

I didn't go to the wedding.

Shoeshine Girl

'Next!' said the clerk. 'Name?' she said, as Julie sat down. 'First claim?' she went on, as she wrote SUMMERS, JULIE in capitals on a form. 'Date of birth? Address? School leaver, are you?'

Julie nodded.

'You're not eligible for any money until September.'

Julie didn't understand. She thought the £17.30 she'd expected was little enough, but what would she do with nothing?

'Come back the first Monday after term starts.'

'But it's only the middle of July and I'm unemployed – what am I supposed to do?'

The clerk had seen hundreds of teenagers coming in, more every year. At first it had upset her. She had thought, well, they're unemployed and they should get benefits. But she had become accustomed to the routine and went on writing as Julie sat there, dazed.

'Try the job centre,' the clerk said, pausing briefly from her paperwork and looking up at Julie. 'Next!'

As she walked along the street, Julie thought about child benefit. She thought she had ceased to be a child when she had walked through the school gates for the last time at four o'clock the previous Friday.

Nobody even pretended to make the job centre look inviting. It was lit with strip lights and there were dying

34

plants on the window sills. The carpet was brown, the walls were beige, everything was lifeless, listless. There were display stands with brown boards on them and cards pinned to the boards. Welcome to the world of work, thought Julie. Julie heaved herself out of her momentary lethargy. Her spirits rose a little – there seemed to be plenty of jobs. Jobs for typists, joiners, builders, skilled labourers, nothing for school leavers. Then she saw one for a trainee sales assistant in a record shop. That would be good, she thought, you could play music all day. She got out her biro to make a note and then saw the small print: 'Graduate preferred'. Her spirits wilted and she read on: plumber, bricklayer, chef . . . Then something caught her eye:

Job: Shoeshine girl
District: Leeds/London Inter City trains
Wages: £42 per week
Hours: Negotiable
Details: Girl needed for Inter City personal shoeshining service. Uniform, equipment, fares, LVs, full training given.
(Excepted vacancy – Sex Discrimination Act.)

At least you'd be on the move, she thought. And go to London every day. She wondered why it had to be a girl but didn't dwell on that too much.

Julie put on her best skirt and blouse. Crossing her fingers, she set off for the interview that had been arranged for her by the job centre. The office was in a seedy building off the main street in Leeds city centre. She stood outside the door looking at the name embossed on the opaque glass door. 'Wilfred Bottomley, Employment Agent.' She suppressed a smile at the name Bottomley. A little man poked his shiny head around the door.

'Miss Summers?' he said. Julie nodded. 'Come in.'

He pointed to a chair in front of his large, shabby desk. A glance was enough to show that there had never been splendour in that office.

'Now then Miss Summers, this is a brand new service we are starting for the Inter City and we are looking for a presentable and capable young woman for this excellent job with very good prospects. Our customers will want their shoes nice and shiny as many of them will be important businessmen who haven't got time for sloppy work or gossiping girls.' He peered at her through thick glasses. 'What age are you?'

'Seventeen,' Julie replied.

'Hmm, a bit on the young side. 'O' levels?'

'English Language and Maths, and I've just taken three more.'

'Good, we are looking for a properly educated girl.'

He was looking at her, his eyes resting momentarily on her legs and then on her chest. Julie felt as though she was squirming, but in fact she was sitting rigidly still and bolt upright. Mr Bottomley finished his inspection and cleared his throat.

'Now then, the work is hard. No slackers. No time for a shirker in this job I can tell you. You start on the 7 a.m. commuter train. I am looking for a girl with the dedication to do overtime and come back on the train that gets in at 9 p.m. That's four trains, an hour for lunch with LVs.' He paused for effect.

'I'm not prepared to take on anyone who won't do those hours.'

He took off his spectacles and wiped them with a grubby handkerchief.

'There's plenty of girls just dying for an opportunity like this.'

A long day, thought Julie, but variety after all.

'Now then,' he began again. She wished he wouldn't say 'Now then' so much.

'Let's have a good look at you. Smile please.' He laced his waxy, stubby fingers through each other. Julie's face froze.

'Come along, all the applicants have to do this, our clients don't want someone shining their shoes who never smiles, do they?' There are hundreds of girls better qualified than you who would give an arm and a leg for this job, oh yes, arm and a leg.' Julie thought of all the arms and legs they'd have to cut off and saw them piled up outside the door of his office and the thought made her smile because it was so ridiculous.

'That's better.' Encouraged by her smile Mr Bottomley pressed on. 'Walk to the door and back please.'

The smile vanished. Julies knees felt tightly locked like in nightmares. 'Now then, walk to the door please,' Mr Bottomley said, snappily. 'I don't need to remind you of the thousands of youngsters out there who'd do anything for a career break like this – travel, meet people, see Britain – come along, just to the door and back, I haven't got all day.'

Appalled as she was, Julie forced herself to get up. She walked to the door and back feeling exposed and wretched. She thought of all the orders obeyed by all the children and young people all over the world. She sat down again. He made some notes, muttering as he did so. 'Not exactly Miss World, but then that's not what we need is it?' He scribbled and mumbled, 'Nice straight teeth . . . presentable . . .' He looked up. 'Adequate, quite adequate,' he said. He slid a small suitcase out from under his desk.

'Now then, the equipment.' He showed her each brush and tin as though displaying rare antiques. 'Now then, let's

see you shine my shoes.' Julie hesitated, feeling humiliated
by his power to order her to display herself, first in one way
then in another.

'Come along, girl! Time is one thing I do not have to
waste!'

Reluctantly, Julie went to his side of the desk and knelt
down. She put the shoe board in front of him and he lifted
his foot onto it.

'If the client doesn't put his foot on the board, you must
lift it gently by the ankle and place it on the board.' He
removed his foot. 'Do that.' Julie lifted his pudgy ankle
onto the board secretly wincing.

'Now then, select the brush and polish and give the shoe
a good once over for my money.'

Julie did as she was told, her head was down and the
little man peered at her. She could feel his fishy little eyes
on her but didn't look up. He was looking down her shirt at
her breasts.

'Good,' he said. 'You may return to your seat. Now then
you will be charging each customer 75p and I shall expect
you to bring back at least £20 a day. Any discrepancies or
less than that amount and I shall have no trouble in finding
someone with more flair and talent. Is that clear? You can
start tomorrow.'

Julie wondered about the hundreds of talented girls
who'd give their arms and legs for the job. How come she'd
got it so quickly?

'Times are hard,' said Mr Bottomley as if reading her
thoughts. 'And we none of us can be choosers these days.'

Julie thought of her wage, £42 a week. He's making a lot
more out of this than I am, she realized. And then she
heard his voice again, 'Can't be choosers'. She thought of
the job centre and the dole office.

'I'll take the job.'

Mr Bottomley awarded her with a smile which looked as if it were kept for special occasions: ceremonies, weddings and funerals.

'And so, now the uniform,' he said and went over to a wardrobe. He took out a hanger on which hung a brown checked shirt, a short open-fronted jacket and a straight brown skirt.

'Slip into the Ladies and try this on now would you, Miss Summers?' He handed her the suit.

He held the door open and pointed down the corridor to the Ladies. The brown lino squeaked as she walked along feeling very strange. It was a tiny, grim Ladies with broken wire-glass in the window and a fern growing on the damp wall outside. She struggled into the clothes. She went back to the office, her own clothes under her arm. Mr Bottomley looked at her as a purveyor of meats might cast his eye over a side of beef. As he looked, he took the bundle of her clothes from under her arm. This made Julie feel curiously naked, robbed of her identity.

'Very nice. My word, what an improvement,' he said. Julie glanced at him half expecting to see the wedding and funeral smile. But his shiny little face was unsmiling. Julie felt as though automatic reflexes had taken over. He opened the wardrobe door and instructed her to look in the mirror. She glanced at herself, she didn't know what to think. The skirt was a bit tight, she thought. And then she saw his reflection. He was standing behind her looking her up and down. She returned to her chair.

He sat behind his desk shuffling papers in a show of importance and handed her a plastic folder. 'This carries your train timetable and pass. I have filled in your name, please sign here before starting work. There are a week's supply of LVs, a clipboard and forms to be signed by clients. I want each client to sign a form.' He looked at her hard. 'I find honesty is essential in life.'

Julie looked at him and felt she had aged ten years.
Words like honesty turned to pulp and lost their meaning
coming out of this man's mouth.

'Now then, one or two points,' he continued. 'You may
accept tips but you are not to solicit them. He lingered
slightly on the word 'solicit' and although Julie wasn't sure
what the word meant, she guessed. She had a flash of
herself caressing the ankles of businessmen in an effort
to get tips and was horrified. Where did such thoughts
come from?

'The uniform must be clean at all times and keeping it
that way is your responsibility. Don't bring me dry cleaning bills.'

Julie looked at Mr Bottomley. She imagined that bosses
were a class of people who were cleancut and suave, people
with an air of authority emanating from expensive clothes
and perfectly manicured demeanour. Mr Bottomley was
greasy and dumpy and there emanated from him ill-
concealed irritation and a festering resentment.

'You're a very lucky girl,' he droned on. 'Thousands
would . . .' Julie fixed a smile on her face so that she
wouldn't have to listen.

At 6.45 a.m. the next morning, Julie stood on a platform at
Leeds Central, looking at the commuters pacing backwards and forwards glancing at their watches. She was very
nervous. She turned over every possible opening phrase:
'Excuse me sir, would you like your shoes shone? Shined?
Polished? Cleaned? The train pulled into the station and
the commuters made a rush for the doors. There was
something ruthless and alarming about the speed with
which they made for the train and pushed their way onto it.
They headed for specific seats as though they belonged to

them. Julie waited in the corridor space between two first-class carriages, watching her potential customers. She panicked when it struck her that she would only be able to shine the shoes of those sitting on the outside. There was no way she was crawling under the tables to reach the passengers sitting by the windows. Why hadn't Mr Bottomley mentioned that? Julie pressed her face to the window as the train moved out of the station, wishing she was anywhere else but where she was. She made a big effort, told herself she'd better wise up and get on with it. She peered into a carriage. The passengers were almost all men and most of them were disappearing behind newspapers or settling down to sleep. She'd just have to begin, there was no way round it.

'Excuse me,' she said shyly to a passenger by the door. He looked up at her crossly. 'Excuse me . . . I'm sorry . . . I . . . I, well . . . I . . .' He glared at her even harder. 'Would you, um, would you . . . would you like me to clean your shoes for you . . . sir?' He stared at her in amazement. He peered down at his shoes and then back at her and grunted. Then he raised his newspaper and shook it straight in order to block her out. One or two others watched this little scene. She turned and fled to the next carriage, overcome with embarrassment. Luckily it was a carriage of closed compartments which would make the kneeling down easier – that is, if anyone agreed to having their shoes cleaned.

She tapped on the door and slid it open, bungling in with her box and clipboard. The three passengers looked up and she said, 'Would you like your shoes cleaned?' She heard her voice as though it were someone else's. She looked from one to the other of them. One of them smiled and said, 'That's a good idea – how much?' He seemed to think 75p was reasonable, and she knelt down to clean his shoes, relieved to have her first customer. She selected the polish and began the brushing. She got out the duster and buff and polished the shoes. Just for a moment she had an overwhelming desire to cry. She felt vulnerable and diminished. When she had finished and got her first client's signature, another asked her if she would do his shoes. With two signatures and £1.50 in her pocket she felt a little better. She moved through the carriages, developing a kind of numbness that helped to separate her from this work.

At King's Cross Julie got off the train with the commuters and wandered around. She liked the hurrying and business of the big station. She sat in the buffet and had tea and sandwiches. She looked in the little kiosks and noticed that a lot of pigeons in London had deformed feet. She went down into the tunnels leading to the tube station out of curiosity more than anything and was impressed by the singer with a guitar whose voice filled the long passageway beneath the ground. She thought times must be really hard for everybody if someone who could play the guitar and sing so well had to beg with his jacket on the ground to catch pennies. She kept an eye on the time and caught her next train. And so it went until the end of the week, without any remarkable mistakes or nastiness. By the Friday she was beginning to be familiar with the routine, and one or two of the commuters recognized her. Mr Bottomley was pleased with the results and congratulated her, not forgetting to warn her that beginners' luck doesn't ensure permanent success and there were hundreds like her who'd give their eye teeth for such a marvellous opportunity. Eye teeth, thought Julie, and arms and legs.

The second week began just like the first. Julie watched the commuters, ordinary men in suits carrying Samsonite briefcases, temporarily behaving like piranhas swarming for the train and then once in their seats becoming human again, respectable, wrapped in shirts and ties, sitting quietly in their seats.

She began to recognize faces at King's Cross, some of the buffet staff, one or two ticket collectors. There was also an ageing woman in an old coat, her hair ragged and matted, her legs bare, purple and blotchy, with feet in men's shoes several sizes too big, who drifted around the station raving. Some days she raved noisily, others she just muttered to herself, looking around suddenly and directing her gaze either angry or blank, at some random passerby. Julie always felt she should speak to her but never knew how to or had the nerve to. She noticed there were also a number of girls of her age; she saw them on trains and in the station. She saw the masks they wore, make-up to give them courage, a false boldness in their eyes. She observed a certain kind of man who hung around the station trying to look as if they had some reason for being there but keeping a sharp eye on the law. They watched the young girls. Julie was frightened of them. There was another man lurking who she didn't notice.

On nice days, she sometimes sat on a bench in the station, watching the people go by and eating her sandwiches. Sometimes she read her favourite magazines. One Friday, just before the afternoon train back to Leeds, Julie sat reading her magazine, absorbed in the serial. A smartly dressed man sat on another bench nearby, looking at her surreptitiously from behind his newspaper. What he didn't see was someone watching him, a girl with short bright auburn hair sticking up from her head, wearing tight jeans and high-heeled boots. She was chewing gum, leaning against the side of a snacks kiosk and gently tapping her leg with a rolled up magazine. Her eyes were narrowed with contempt. The man lit a long cigarette with a gold lighter and as he inhaled, he looked more closely at Julie eating her sandwiches and reading her magazine. The girl also looked at Julie. She knew what was going on. She sized Julie up as different from the ones with their mascara and rouge masks, their fear accentuated rather than concealed by their red lipstick. Julie was more innocent than they were, unsuspicious and vulnerable. What an idiot, thought the auburn-haired girl. Sitting there like that all innocent, just the way she was when he'd found her. Except that she hadn't been wearing a daft brown suit and carrying around what appeared to be a shoeshine kit. Oh, leave it be, the girl told herself, it's none of my business.

The man returned to his newspaper and then glanced at his watch. The auburn-haired girl shifted her weight and suddenly dodged behind the kiosk out of sight as the man got up, carefully folding the paper and smoothing down his jacket. He strolled towards the platform for the Leeds train. The girl watched as Julie wiped her mouth with the back of her hand and put her magazine in the shoeshine kit box. She too got up and went towards the Leeds train. The girl watched the man slow down, let Julie pass and look her up and down as she got into the train, still oblivious of him. Then he too boarded the train. Something snapped in the girl's mind. She made a resolution. She swung her bag over her shoulder and strode off towards the street.

Julie went into a closed compartment, sliding the door open without really thinking. There was only one man in there. He looked up. Would he like his shoes cleaned? Yes. He was very well dressed and wore very expensive shoes. Julie was beginning to think she could tell what people were like by their shoes. There was something instantly unsettling about this man, but she didn't know what. His shoes were top-price Bond Street Italian leather. Money,

she thought. She had a sense that there was also something street sharp about him. Someone else came in.
He fumbled with the door but Julie didn't look round. Her
customer sat back and watched her as she worked. He
slipped a pound in her pocket, leaning so close that she
could feel his breath on her neck. 'An attractive girl like
you could make a much better living,' he said very softly.
She concentrated hard on the shoes. When she'd finished
she asked him to sign, she didn't look straight at him but
was aware of his good looks. As she turned to go she saw the
fumbling newcomer, a white stick propped against his
knees. The handsome man gently took hold of her wrist
and pulled her towards him. 'I'll keep an eye out for you,'
he whispered. Julie backed away, knocking the blind man's
stick over. He groped for it and she apologized.

For the rest of the journey Julie tried without success to
shake off the unease she felt after the episode with the
smooth man. She was glad that Mr Bottomley had let her
off the last two trains that day since she'd worked three
weekends. Not, he pointed out, that he would be making a
habit of this leniency. It was 4 o'clock, and Julie dashed
from the train as fast as she could to avoid the man.

The bus stop was crowded with noisy flocks of schoolkids.
A tramp rifled through a nearby bin and a boy flicked his
chocolate wrapper at him. Julie sighed. She got off at the
usual stop and walked the fifteen minutes along the high
street. Past the arcade with the space invaders whirring
and thudding, her face set blank against the probable
taunts or invitations from bored boys hanging around the
doorway and showing off to their pals. Past the steamed-up
launderette full of people heaving and humping baskets of
washing. Past the TV rental shop – twenty screens all
showing a woman with a blue rinse remonstrating with a

bald man who gestured with his hands as if to say, Why me?
Familiar scenes, an ordinary normal life. Julie found it
depressing. She didn't want to go home, more of the same.
She drifted into the high street café and saw a group of girls
she knew sitting round a table chatting, smoking and
drinking tea. She joined them. They asked her what she
was up to.

'Going back for 'A's Julie?' asked one.

'No, what's the point?'

'That's what I told my dad and he says, you'll go back if
it's over my dead body my girl!' said another girl.

'Oh they always say that – I told them I've had enough,
and they only went to see the careers teacher themselves,
didn't they?' another girl said. She was 17 and wore a cross
in one ear and a ban-the-bomb badge in the other. Julie
was intrigued by her elaborate make-up. 'I said,' she went
on, 'careers teachers all say the same things and besides,
every job you go for, you're just a number aren't you?
Number 378, not Marlene O'Brien.' She laughed. She
looked at Julie. 'You're working aren't you?' Julie nodded,
suddenly embarrassed. She was the only one of the group
of five or six who had a job.

'I'm doing a job on the trains, going to London every
day.'

'That must be great!' said Marlene, leaning over the
table, her face in her hands. 'London!' Julie thought of
the girls in the station and looked at Marlene who despite
her disguise was no more sophisticated than she was. Julie
smiled and said, 'I thought it would be, but I don't know
really.' And she left it at that before they found out she was
shining shoes for a living.

She opened the door to her family's house and went into
the living-room. Her father was watching TV.

'Home Julie, are you?' he said without looking away from

the TV. 'So what's new then?' He always said this and it always made Julie feel depressed. He had been out of work for over a year and the strain was beginning to make life intolerable. Sometimes he went out and got blind drunk and came home and wept like a child. Julie felt very sympathetic to him but she was horrified seeing a grown man, her father, so broken down. She looked at her dad, feeling sorry for him, but also impatient, wishing he would snap out of his moods. There was a basket of damp washing on the floor. Her mother must have left it there before going out to work. Julie took it into the kitchen and out into the small back yard. It was a drizzly, British summer day. She hung the damp washing on the line in the damp air and wondered if life would always be like this? Her mother worked overtime all the time, cleaning in an office block and working afternoons in a launderette just to keep the household going. She was worn out but didn't allow herself to complain. The sight of her husband dumping himself in the same chair every day drove her to the edge of fury but she bit back her anger, always telling herself it wasn't his fault. He had tried everything, there just wasn't any work for him. He brooded over the horses, repeating the names he fancied as though the repetition might bring him some luck. Julie's brothers, sixteen-year-old Billy and nineteen-year-old David teased her endlessly about her job, always sticking out their feet and asking, 'Hey shoeshine girl what about me?' Then they'd half kill themselves laughing. Bizarre as her job was and ashamed as she was of it, for Julie it was at least a refuge from the claustrophobic oppressiveness of home. But she wasn't quite ready to leave. She wanted to help her mother and she enjoyed the company of her little twin sisters Sue and Jo.

Julie stood in front of the mirror in the ladies at King's Cross combing her thick shoulder-length brown hair. Beside her was the auburn-haired girl. Julie glanced at her, she looked about twenty-one, Julie thought, and she was attractive, unusual. She was stretching her mouth and smoothing on bright lipstick. Her hand slipped and she got a big smudge all over one corner of her mouth. She stood back momentarily and cursed, then she laughed and caught Julie's eye. Ruffling her hair back she said, 'Got to laugh, haven't you?' She had a low, earthy voice. Julie looked at her. She was taller and stronger than Julie and wore tight jeans and high-heeled boots. She was confident and bold. She noticed Julie looking at her and smiled. Julie smiled back.

'What's your name?' she asked Julie. 'Mine's Sandra.'

Julie introduced herself and put away her comb. She felt plain and young and tugged at her sleeves trying to hide her freckled arms. Sandra put away her lipstick and pulled at her jeans to get comfortable. Julie noticed Sandra's eyes, green and slanting. Wise eyes, thought Julie, bet she doesn't miss a thing. Sandra swung her bag over her shoulder and turned to go. Julie was on her way out as well. They managed to knock into each other and laughed. Julie said goodbye and made for the snacks kiosk to get a can of coke. Sandra did too. 'Good idea, I'll join you,' she said, shoving her money over the counter. They walked over to a bench together drinking through straws. The pigeons bobbed around them waiting for crumbs and Julie looked at their feet again.

'Why do pigeons in London have deformed feet?' Julie said.

'London's like that,' said Sandra. 'Surprising their wings don't fall off. Where are you from?'

'Leeds,' Julie replied.

'Thought you were from up north,' she said. They sucked on their straws. 'What do you do then?' asked Sandra who already had a fair idea. Julie looked embarrassed. She didn't want to tell her new friend. She instinctively liked Sandra and was ashamed to tell her about the shoeshining. Sandra sat back, one leg propped over the other, ankle on knee. Everything about her expressed defiance, Julie thought. Sandra looked around and Julie thought how bold to scan the surroundings so openly. Then Sandra looked at Julie. She smiled. Sandra had a wonderful smile and a gap between her front teeth. She had a lot of nerve, a lot of cheek, Julie thought.

'So, what do you do I said?' Sandra repeated. She could tell that Julie was reluctant to say.

'I work on the trains,' said Julie looking down and shoving a sweet wrapper round between her toes.

'What as?' You don't exactly look like a guard or a driver – what's your uniform? And the box?'

'I got the box from my boss, Mr Bottomley.'

'Is he really called Bottomley?' Sandra asked, laughing. 'The word bottom or anything like it, Bottomley, always makes me laugh,' she went on. She had a very infectious laugh. Julie found herself smiling too. Her embarrassment was ebbing away.

'Yes, he's called Wilfred Bottomley.'

'Wilfred?!'

'And he says, "Now then" all the time and says lots of girls would give their arms and legs for this job.' Sandra offered Julie a cigarette. Julie declined. She'd never liked them, having once tried in a bike shed when she was 13 and nearly choked to death.

'So what do you do for this Wilfred Bottomley?'

'I shine shoes,' Julie replied, embarrassed again.

'Just left school have you?'

'Yes.'

'Got 'O' levels?'

'Yes, two so far and waiting for results.'

'You leave school with 'O' levels and shine shoes – what a world.' Sandra sighed.

Julie misinterpreted her reaction and grew defensive. 'It's better than sitting in cafes all day.' Perhaps Sandra thought she was a sucker.

'Hey! I only mean you deserve better than that for a start in the world after school. Life after 'O' levels . . .' she smiled and Julie relaxed. Julie thought how hard it was sometimes when you first get to know people you think you like.

'What do you do?'

'Oh this and that,' Sandra waved her hand rather vaguely and drew on her cigarette.

'This and that what?'

'Ducking and diving, scheming and planning.'

Julie didn't like to seem ignorant so she didn't ask for any explanation. They might be London terms for something. She just said 'Oh' and wondered if Marlene or one of the others would be able to tell her what ducking and diving meant.

'What are you doing in the station?' Julie asked without a trace of suspicion.

'I live round here and just come in for a packet of fags now and again, or a magazine. Besides, I like stations, they're full of life aren't they?' There was truth in this. Sandra liked the hubbub of stations, markets, parks on a hot Sunday. She liked people and fun and noise. She gave Julie no hint of any motive beyond the most superficial and plausible.

'Well, I'd better be going, got to get the next train.'

'So you have to go up and down the train shining shoes?'

Julie nodded as she packed her bits and pieces into her box.

'All men I suppose?' said Sandra.

'Yes, so far.'

'Yeah, well, men.' Sandra's tone was loaded. Julie remembered the remark after she'd gone but didn't think about it too hard.

'I'll be back down tomorrow,' said Julie. She wanted to ask Sandra to sit and chat with her again but lacked the confidence to ask her.

Sandra stretched and yawned. She grinned at Julie. She got up and said, 'See you kid,' and swaggered off. Julie watched her go, admiring the insolent way she walked, kind of kicking the pavement as she went.

Julie picked up her box and walked in the direction of the platform. As the train pulled out, she thought about Sandra, about the way you sometimes met people and instantly liked them almost as though you recognized them but you'd actually never met them before. She liked Sandra's way of being tough but warm and friendly, sharp but kind. She hoped she'd see her again but thought why would someone like Sandra want to be friends with someone plain like her.

She knelt in front of the customers feeling tired and bored. There must be some other way to earn a living. She packed up the box and as she passed an empty compartment decided to have a rest. She watched the fields streak past and was lost in thought when the door slid open and someone came in. It was the blind man. He tapped into the carriage and sat down. He was neat and proud and about fifty, Julie guessed. He just sat there very still and she looked at him. She was surprised when he spoke to her thinking he couldn't know there was anyone in the carriage.

'Who are you?' he said and before she could reply he

said, 'Are you the shoeshine girl?' She nodded and then realized that was no use to him.

'Yes, I am,' she replied.

'That must be a hard job for a young girl.' He smiled kindly.

'Yes, it is,' she said.

'And you have to be careful,' he said, 'avoid men like the one whose shoes you were doing yesterday.'

Julie wondered how he knew so much. She was alarmed by what he said but at the same time she found his presence soothing. She offered to clean his shoes for free.

'No favours, thank you,' he said kindly. His dignity impressed her. She sighed, regretting that she had to go and shine a few more shoes or face the wrath of Mr Bottomley and his barrage of speeches.

'I'd better go,' she said, 'thanks for . . .' she wasn't sure what to thank him for so she touched his arm in farewell and left.

'Shoe shine, shoe shine, shine my shoes,' said Patrick as she opened the door.

'Oh give over, I'm tired.'

'Lost your sense of humour have you?' said Patrick. She scowled at him.

'Lend us a fiver Julie,' said Patrick. She refused. He was always borrowing from her mother and never paid her back.

She went into the kitchen. Her little sisters were playing with wooden spoons. They were hitting each other and soon there'd be tears. Her mother was sitting in the last of the evening light admiring the runner beans she was growing in a tub. A quiet scene, a normal family, Julie smiled. It wasn't always so bad. She sat on the ground by her mother, leaning her head against her mother's knees. Her mother gently stroked her hair. Julie thought of the last week. She saw Sandra, the blind man, and the smooth-talking handsome man. 'An attractive girl like you could make a much better living.' Julie blocked her mind from understanding without even being conscious that she was doing so. But the memories didn't go away. She heard Sandra's voice, 'Ducking and diving.' She heard the blind man: 'Avoid men like . . .' She felt as though she were drifting on a tide she couldn't resist and she had an urge to cling to her mother. Something held her back from trying to express these feelings; they were like dreams, shadowy and sharp and fleeting.

Monday morning, 6.45 a.m. – the usual display of savagery as the commuters fought for their seats, the clash of Samsonite briefcases as they squeezed through doors teeth practically bared, shoving into one another. Julie started her rounds. The train swooshed past suburbs and through fields. She was walking along a corridor when there was a tap on the window of a compartment. She looked round. It was the smooth handsome man. He slid the door open and asked her to shine his shoes. There was something about him, some force, some persuasiveness that she didn't like or trust but found hard to resist. As he lifted his foot onto the board he said, 'Don't you get tired of feet and shoes?' She nodded but kept her head down working at his pricey shoes. There were two other men in the compartment, one was dozing, the other hidden behind a newspaper. The man leaned over as he had before and whispered almost into Julie's neck, 'I told you, an attractive young girl like you could make a much better living.' She kept polishing the shoes until they were so shiny she could almost see her face in them, like the distorted reflection in the back of a spoon only darkened. 'I could help you you know,' he breathed. Julie dreaded standing up and having to talk to him. Her heart was beating hard. She got up swiftly and packed her things away trying to break his menacing spell. She dropped a brush and a tin of polish which he deftly retrieved and slipped into her box and as she turned to go, still without looking at him and not taking his money, he slipped a five pound note and a piece of paper with a name and telephone number on it into her pocket. Julie wanted to return them but the man who had been dozing was awake and she didn't want anyone to see.

When the train pulled into King's Cross Julie got off it as fast as she could to avoid the smooth-talking man. She nearly ran along the platform making for the buffet. She didn't see Sandra standing behind a pillar, a pile of mail bags beside her. Sandra watched the people getting off the train as she had before. She saw Julie and witnessed her panic. He got off the train just after Julie, who didn't look back but hurried along. The man fixed his gaze on Julie. He didn't see Sandra whose expression changed from contempt to hard resolve. He wouldn't get away with it again. Sandra tracked him as he followed Julie. Julie didn't go straight to the buffet as she usually did, but seemed to change her mind and head for the Ladies, weaving through the early morning crowd amidst the noise and bustle and endless announcements. He weaved after her but when she went into the Ladies he looked at his watch. He seemed to be weighing something up. Sandra knew his expressions well. She kept out of his sight but went dangerously close. He hesitated and turned away towards the exit and the taxi queue. He could have been any business-man starting his week in the capital city.

Julie came out of the Ladies and made for the buffet. She was starving and ordered three rounds of toast and two cups of tea. With her mouth full of toast she looked round, hoping she might see Sandra, but suspecting that anyway it was a bit early for someone like Sandra. There were two girls her age at separate tables. It was a dark stormy morning and their faces were unnaturally bright against the strip lighting. Their eyes were heavy with make-up, kohl pencil and mascara. Runaways, thought Julie, girls looking for work and excitement, life, escape from their families. Girls with no street sense – yet. Girls who'd planned and packed, leaving a note in their best writing, and fled with a couple of quid and crazed, desperate hopes. Julie thought of pictures in newspapers and on posters of missing teenagers.

Sandra swung herself into the chair opposite Julie. 'Watcher.'

'Hello,' said Julie with her mouth full. Sandra smiled.

'Hungry work? How's life? How's shoes?'

'OK, same as usual.' She didn't want to mention the man.

'Nice weekend?'

'Yeah, well, same as usual. My little sisters had this big fight over a doll. It drinks and you know, well . . . pees. Well, one of them gives it ketchup and its ducts get blocked so the other one cuts its hair and then there's a huge fight. They're only seven!'

'Kids!' Sandra smiled.

'How about you?' Julie paused, 'been ducking and diving?'

It was an innocent question, but, thought Sandra, the maddening thing about the innocent is that sometimes they know, but don't know they know.

'No, had the weekend off with my friend Bev who lives upstairs.'

'Did you go somewhere?'

'Yeah, took the kids to the funfair.'

'Kids? Have you got kids?'

'I've got one, he's three, Bev's got two, they're three and four.'

Julie stared at her wide eyed. 'How old are you?'

'Twenty-one. Anyway, so what?' Sandra felt impatient.

'Sorry, I just thought . . . well . . . are you married?'

'No – do I look like the married sort?'

'Well, not exactly.'

'Have you got a fella?' Sandra asked.

'No,' Julie replied ashamed because she'd never been out with a boy or even kissed one properly. 'Have you?'

'Did have, but he gave me a hard time. I try to keep away from him but it's not always that easy.'

'Why?'

'Well . . .'

'Sandra what is ducking and diving?'

'Do you really not know?'

'No.'

'Can't you work it out? See those girls.' She indicated the ones with the make-up and the frightened, false bold eyes. 'They come from small towns like me, towns where nothing happens and there's no work, people look like they're dying on their feet. That kind of place. So they come to big cities looking for something.' Sandra thought Julie must have worked it out by now.

'I still don't understand what it is you do. Is it shop lifting?' Julie found the thought shocking.

'No,' said Sandra sighing, half amused, half irritated.

'What then?'

'It's bad. But it pays. And I never want to be poor again, never.'

'What is it? Oh Sandra, not . . .'

'Yes, prostitution, the game.'

Julie went pale and rigid. She was really shocked. Sandra

was a prostitute! Someone she liked and wanted to be
friends with was a prostitute. 'How could you?' she burst
out passionately, upset because she liked her so much.

'Listen kid, don't go all moral and hoity toity on me will
you? Because I can do without it. See those kids with the
faces? They'll be doing it soon if they don't wise up fast and
go home on the next train. I'd tell them but they wouldn't
listen.'

Julie shook her head. 'But how can you?'

'Look,' Sandra was getting angry, beginning to wonder
how she'd let herself go soft and resolved to save the stupid
kid from him. Let her get caught, then she'd have to give
up her high and mighty moral tones. 'Look, I like you and
I don't want to upset you but when you come from where I
do you don't have that much choice, see?'

'Where do you come from?'

'Just out of London somewhere, like I said, nowhere,
just a small town. My dad was out of work, my mum was in
and out of depressions. I didn't get on with my brothers,
my older sister was married to a man that beat her and
always coming home with her bruises and her three kids
and my younger sisters were tearaways . . . it was hell.
I couldn't find work except in a launderette, 75p an hour.
Couldn't stand it. So one day I just took a few things and
left. I was going to be a model. I send them a postcard now
and then, and some money. I tell them I'm temping. They
don't know about Charly.'

'Charly?'

'My kid.'

'But how can you?' said Julie, mildly now, bewildered.

'I don't need religious lectures or anything you know.
How can I? Because I got conned into it and now I'm in it
and it pays and I'm trying to get out but it's not that easy.
Charly's dad makes sure of that. I'm going to make my

fortune and save it and then me and Bev are getting out,
going to buy a house in the country. Have chickens and
pigs . . .'

Julie looked at Sandra, and couldn't find it in her to sit in
judgement over her. She understood. Or thought she did.
Sandra wasn't going to tell her about the man, that was
her private battle. 'Hey, Sandra, sorry, I was shocked,
I still am,' she smiled bravely. 'But I like you too.' The two
girls looked at each other feeling emotions neither could
express.

Regaining her nerve and zest, Sandra got up and said,
'Lunch tomorrow? Come and see my palace and meet Bev
and the kids.'

'OK,' said Julie, amazed that she still liked Sandra after
her revelation.

Julie turned her key in the lock, feeling particularly tired
after her day's work. She heard the sound of voices raised
in anger which made her want to back out again. Her
parents had started having terrible rows almost every
night after her mother got home. They argued about the
washing-up and the cleaning. He wouldn't do any. But she
was the breadwinner. Did he think she wanted to spend
her life going from one cleaning job to the next and then
come home and clean and wash and cook? Did he? And did
she think it was fun for him every day stuck in the house
with no work and no money? Did she? The twins began to
wail. Julie's urge to leave had been growing steadily. The
row subsided. She heard the door bang and her father go
out. Julie went downstairs and found her mother in the
kitchen with her head in her hands. She put her arm round
her mother.

'Oh Julie, I don't want it to be like this for you, this isn't
how I imagined things would be.'

Sandra hadn't yet told her friend Bev about her plan. It had become almost an obsession with her. She would save Julie from the man. She concealed herself behind the pillar she had used before as Julie's train came in. He wasn't on it. Perhaps he'd gone off somewhere. He regularly did since he had business interests that took him to foreign cities. Sandra had a good idea what they were; his was the world of drugs and flesh. She shuddered thinking about the time she'd spent with him, under his spell. Julie got off the train in her funny brown suit and Sandra smiled. She walked over to her and fell into step beside her. 'Hi, we're having lunch at my place, remember?'

Julie was a bit startled and conflicting feelings raced through her mind. But she's a prostitute! I can't go to her house! I might get into trouble . . . suppose she wants me to . . . no! She couldn't. She's my friend . . . I like her. The thoughts rested there and Julie smiled. 'Yes, let's go to your place.'

Sandra hooked her arm through Julie's and led her through the station. Like the sweep of a beam of light scanning the horizons, she surveyed her surroundings. This was done nonchalantly as though whatever she saw would make no difference anyway. But she didn't miss a thing.

Sandra led Julie to the line of cabs outside the station and they got in. 'May as well travel in style!' she said. Julie hadn't been in a London taxi before and she loved it. It wasn't a long ride. They stopped at the foot of a sky scraper. Sandra gave the taxi driver a big tip and he smiled appreciatively at her. She looked over her shoulder at him. 'Can't take it with you can you?' She laughed.

The lift smelled. The walls were dirty grey metal covered in grafitti, most of it obscene. Sandra lived on the tenth floor. She twisted a fat key in one lock and a thinner one in a second. 'Lot of funny people around, got to be careful. Still, lucky to get housed at all, it was because I had a kid.'

There were three rooms, two poky bedrooms and a larger living room. There were toys and clothes everywhere. It was a tip, but a nice tip. Sandra put on a record and clicked her fingers and danced a bit as she opened a cupboard and took out a bottle of vodka and two glasses. 'Let's drink to your arrival in the big city! Your first visit to my place!' Julie didn't want to seem naive and childish so she accepted a drink. She didn't like alcohol it made her head feel as though it were a long way from her shoulders. She sipped her drink, suppressing a grimace. She wished it was all orange and no vodka, but that wasn't the way Sandra mixed a drink. Sandra looked at her. 'You haven't lived have you?' she said. Julie sipped her drink.

'Where's your kid?' she asked Sandra.

'Upstairs with Bev, we'll go up and get him later and you can meet Bev.' Sandra mixed two more drinks and they sat talking for a while. Julie began to feel relaxed, and her head didn't feel several feet above her shoulders. Sandra went into the kitchen and appeared five minutes later with baked beans on toast.

'I said I was going to give you lunch didn't I?' She kicked her shoes off and Julie sunk into a sofa. The vodka bottle was draining away. Julie felt happier than she had for a long time, realizing how much she enjoyed being listened to, warmed by Sandra's interest in her. She missed one train and then another, and then it was Sandra's turn to talk.

'I sat on the station like those dumb kids but not for long. This guy made friends with me, he was handsome and kind and rich. I fell for it.' Sandra didn't tell Julie who the man was. 'I fell for it and then it was too late. I was so hooked on him I did what he wanted me to. At first it was just pictures, then it was worse, finally he threatened me, if I didn't go home with the "gentlemen" as he called them, he'd make sure I never forgot, after all he'd done for me. All the luxury he'd given me, expensive gifts, clothes, housed me in a beautiful flat, took me on continental weekends. I was in love with him. I was that stupid. He said as soon as we'd earned enough, we'd buy a big house in the country and have a swimming pool and I could be happy for ever. He said he loved me. He told me about his tragic past. I fell for it, the whole lot. Can you believe it?'

Sandra drained the last of the vodka. Julie looked at her new friend too shocked to reply. Behind Sandra on the wall was a little picture of her and a little boy with black curly hair, Charly, Julie supposed. They were laughing. 'And then I got pregnant – by him of course, I knew that for sure. I told him, refusing to admit to myself what was going on. I told myself he loved me, he'd be happy, he'd care for me and the baby, I could stop doing what I had to do.' She paused. 'He said "Get an abortion" and I refused. It's all right for women that want them but I didn't want one, I was always sure about that. He said he'd make sure I miscarried. He said it wouldn't hurt much, one kick in my belly and that would be it. He said he hadn't "invested" all this time and money in me just so I could go all soppy about having kids. I couldn't believe it, my lover, the first man I'd ever loved, the one who was so kind. I agreed, I said I'd have the abortion. I knew I had to put on a really good act to convince him of my change of heart, and act I did, for two weeks. I stashed away money and clothes bit by bit with Bev and one day I just didn't go back to him. He's been looking for me ever since but I've managed to avoid him. I know too much and I hate him too much.' She looked at Julie. 'And I've never spoken to anyone about it except Bev. It's a secret. And I never want to talk about it again.'

Evening had come. Julie looked at Sandra, seeing for the

first time how even the toughest and most worldly women can be as vulnerable as children. Sandra shook herself and said 'OK sob story over, enough of this. Let's go and get Charly and you can meet Bev, she's lovely.' She grabbed Julie's hand and dragged her up a flight to Bev's flat. Julie was touched when she saw Sandra with Charly. He clung to her and she nuzzled his neck and kissed him. Bev's kids clamoured around Sandra's legs wanting her attention too.

'Hi, I'm Bev. Like some coffee? I expect she's been plying you with vodka hasn't she?'

They sat in Bev's living room amidst the childrens' chaos drinking coffee and chatting. Julie was happy, really happy. She didn't care about Mr Bottomley and the trains. 'What are you thinking about?' Sandra asked her.

'Oh nothing.'

'I bet you were thinking about Mr Bottomley and how many trains you've missed.' Julie laughed.

'Who the hell's Mr Bottomley?' said Bev.

'My boss. He's awful,' said Julie.

'Stay here if you like,' Sandra said casually. Julie was startled by the offer, yet she also knew she would stay.

'Old Bottomley won't have you back after this anyway.' That was probably true. But what about her mum?

'And you'll be away from all that squabbling in your house.' That was also true.

'You can 'phone your mum.'

'Yeah, go on stay,' said Bev who seemed to be permanently good natured and hospitable, her full brown face framed by a cloud of black hair.

'You can stay here and help me and Bev with the kids. You could even take a couple more in couldn't you? Baby minding. You can stay in my flat, we'll have a good time! Just think Julie, no more shoes!'

Julie was tempted. But what about her mum?

'Don't think too hard,' said Sandra. 'Nothing'll ever change if you do.'

'But what about my mum?'

'Ring her and write to her, and when you've been home to collect your things she'll be used to you being grown up. The dust will settle you'll see. It'll be great!'

Julie felt like a flower filmed in slow motion – the extraordinary way you see them opening out, changes imperceptible to the eye. She saw her family like figures in a dream. She felt she was growing older, that she was beginning to have a past. She looked at Bev and Sandra who were sorting out a scrap between the children and knew she'd never go back to Mr Bottomley, Employment Agent. She thought of her mother with pain, but knew that of all people, her mother would understand. Sandra and Bev went into the kitchen. There was a clattering of pots and pans, a sound Julie loved, something safe and familiar about it. She played with the kids whose initial reserve quickly disappeared.

'Bev, keep clattering the pots, I don't want Julie to hear this.' Bev nodded and busied herself noisily. 'He's back! He's been watching Julie. We've got to keep her away from him.'

'Jesus, Sandra,' Bev whispered holding her friend's arm. 'That means you ought to get out fast.'

Sandra shrugged. 'I'll keep out of his way don't you worry.'

Julie heard their low voices behind the din of the kitchen but thought nothing of it, she felt comforted by them, as if she'd found the older sisters she always wished she'd had.

Bev and Julie worked together. Bev took in another child and they looked after the whole lot of them. Bev and Julie got on well. Julie loved Bev's good humour and instant tempers, burned out as fast as they ignited. She would shout in West Indian dialect and her kids would look at her with huge dark eyes and say yes and thank you and sorry and then she'd wink and hug and kiss them. They took the children to the park or to the playground and on rainy days coped together with the tantrums and restless energy of children who couldn't get out to play.

Days passed. Weeks passed. In the evenings Sandra would sometimes take Julie out to cinemas or discos. Sandra loved dancing. The three of them grew very close. Julie felt suspended in time and space caught in a rhythm of peace that regenerated from day to day, and she didn't let fear of the future blight the happiness she felt. She had occasional lonely moments when she had to fight back a sense of threat she felt waited somewhere in the shadows. Each separately felt this fear in her own way. None of them voiced it, they had their reasons.

One night Sandra came home with champagne. It was Bev's twenty-third birthday. Sandra called her old lady and kissed and hugged her and when the kids were asleep she danced with her while Julie sat watching Bev and Sandra in each others' arms. Julie fell asleep that night on Bev's couch and later Sandra stood over her, tucking a blanket around her sleeping friend. Bev and Sandra had a tacit understanding that this girl would not go through what they had, would not have to face what they had faced. They never said so, but their desire was to protect her innocence, almost as though making up for the mutilation of their own. Bev knew it was only a matter of time before Sandra would be confronted by the smooth man. She dreaded it but could not stop Sandra from living how she chose to, where she chose to. Sandra didn't talk about dodging behind trees and cars and in and out of doorways. Summer was almost over. The days were drawing in and the threat was creeping closer.

'Bitch! Slut! Whore!' He'd caught up with her. Sandra struggled, trying to tear her arm away from his grip. She had just got out of a smart car at the end of a cul-de-sac. The client zipped up his fly and seeing the good-looking man in the smart clothes grabbing the girl he'd just paid, he backed out fast. Sandra fought, but the more she fought the harder he gripped.

'You do as I say or you face the consequences,' he said dangerously.

'Leave me alone,' Sandra said, her teeth clenched. She was trying to fight back her fear.

'Your money is my money and don't you forget it. I taught you everything you know. You owe me a lot and you're my woman. You do what I say and go to the clients I take you to, none of this street walking, only the best hotels and residences, a few films. You do as I say. You won't escape.'

'I hate you, I hate you, you taught me nothing but filth, I hate you with all my heart. Pimp! Dealer! Pusher!' She had gone too far. He twisted her arm so hard it burned. She bit her lips determined not to break down.

'And this is just the beginning,' he said as he hit her fiercely across the face, knocking her to the ground. 'Next time you won't even be able to crawl away,' he said and kicked her in the ribs as she lay on the ground. He walked away straightening his cuffs beneath the expensive suit. Sandra dragged herself over to the wall of a big building nearby. She crouched against it in the dark lonely street and wept.

Julie gasped in horror when she saw Sandra's swollen blackened eyes the next morning. 'Customer got frisky,' said Sandra pouring herself some coffee. 'Happens occasionally. I gave him a slap so he thumped me.' Julie was upset and frightened. 'Oh come on Julie, it happens now and again, don't make a fuss it doesn't hurt, it just looks bad.' Sandra managed to disguise the pain in her ribs and her arm. Julie started to cry. 'Hey, come on, shutup will you kid? No good you crying, if anyone should cry it's me and I'm OK! So shutup will you?' Sandra tried to laugh. She spent the day sleeping and in the evening when Bev and Julie got back from the park, they all watched TV together in Bev's flat. Julie was tired and went down with little Charly and fell asleep.

'You've got to go!' Bev said urgently as soon as Julie was gone.

'I did that before and he found me. Remember? Why should I run away? It's my life here with Charly and you. I'll do what I like!' Sandra hadn't lost any of her defiance but she was badly scared beneath it. Bev could tell. Sandra turned and clung to Bev who put her arms round her, suddenly Sandra wasn't sassy, brave or street-wise, she was crying.

Autumn had arrived and the clocks were about to go back. Julie had taken to reading to the kids and telling them long stories. It was almost as though she sensed the tension rising without letting the realization hit her that this couldn't go on forever. After all, there was no reason why it shouldn't. She lost herself more and more in fantasies and fictions and closed her mind to the passing of time and the rising pressure.

Sandra pulled her collar around her chin and held her jacket close to herself. She shivered. She had avoided being out alone after dark since he had attacked her but he hadn't reappeared. Perhaps he'd been arrested. She hoped they were on to him and his mafia. Surely he couldn't afford to be caught hurting her or anybody else. His little empire would crumble. He had made too many enemies and his

pretty face wouldn't save him when it came to it. Someone
sometime was going to have enough dirt on him and a big
enough grudge to grass him up, she kept telling herself.
It wouldn't be her, she couldn't risk the revenge; she had
Charly and now Julie to think of. She'd saved Julie from
him, that was something, she told herself, and he'd never
get his hands on Charly. She'd kill him first. She strode
along listening to the beats of her heart. She shivered.
Someone was kerb-crawling her. She quickened her pace.
She looked around. There were only a couple of drunks
lumbering along the other side of the road. She began to
run. Footsteps were closing in on her; he must have got out
of the car. The street was deserted and there was a high
cold wind. She turned along an alley, a short-cut she
thought she knew, but in panic she had confused it with
another alley. It was a dead end. She was trapped. She felt
a crack on her head as she went down, down, down.

Julie was alone in Sandra's flat with Charly. He was
playing contentedly. Bev had gone to her mum's and
wouldn't be back until the next day. Charly was up late
because he wanted to see Sandra. He was washed and in
his pyjamas talking to himself quietly as Julie read a book.
Soon Sandra would be home and Charly would go to sleep
and they would sit and chat and have supper. Julie went
into the kitchen and put on some food, enjoying the pots
and pans time of day. The radio was on playing music softly
and Julie felt safe and sound. But Sandra didn't come home
and Charly became fractious. He got worse, becoming
convulsed with sobs, and Julie had to tell him one story
after another to calm him down. Eventually, exhausted he
fell asleep on her lap. Julie put the TV on quietly and
watched until closedown. Sandra had said she'd be back
and although she sometimes went out at night, she always

came home when she said she was going to. Julie began to
feel uneasy. It was the first time she'd been alone for any
length of time without Bev or Sandra. She realized with
growing panic that she had no other friends in London and
she didn't know Bev's mother's address or 'phone number.
The night seemed very long and she jumped every time
she heard a noise, thinking it must be Sandra coming
home. She watched the little button on the TV screen
disappear and quickly turned it off when the close-down
sound wailed at her. Charly shifted and whimpered but he
didn't wake. Julie was very anxious, but still she resisted
the sense of something closing in on her, some threat to
her happiness.

Julie woke with a headache and a dry mouth. She and
Charly had slept on the settee; she was cold and her mouth
felt terrible. Someone was knocking at the door. Muzzy-
headed, she thought, why is Sandra knocking at the door or
is it Bev? But both have keys so why are they knocking?
As the knocking was repeated she emerged from her
sleepiness and remembered that Sandra hadn't come
home the night before. She stumbled over to the door and
opened it to the end of the dream. There was a policeman
and a woman in a fawn mac. Charly began to wail.

'May we come in?' said the policeman. 'This is Sandra
Scammell's flat isn't it?' Julie nodded gathering Charly into
her arms and sitting down with him. The policeman asked
her who she was while the woman in the fawn mac gently
tried to take Charly from her arms, but she held onto
him and he held onto her. Charly was screaming.

'It's for the best,' said the woman, 'I'm from social
services and we'll be looking after little Charly for a while.'

Holding onto him tightly, Julie shouted to the woman to
leave them be.

'Where's Sandra?' her voice had risen. 'Where is she?

Why are you here?' Something made Julie keep talking and shouting, she didn't want to hear bad news. Again the policeman asked her her name and she told him.

'May I ask what relationship you have with Sandra Scammell?' he said.

'I'm her friend. I live here, me and Sandra and Bev from upstairs, we're all friends.

'I'm afraid I have some very bad news for you,' said the policeman. Charly screamed and screamed and Julie held onto him as though onto her own life. The social worker and the policeman led Julie, still holding onto Charly, out of the flat.

One of the neighbours stood by her door, arms folded, saying sniffily to another woman, in a loud whisper, 'I always said it would come to no good.' The social worker had her arm around Julie who was ashen-faced, numb, bewildered.

It rained wildly that day. Julie and Bev stood side by side. Julie had an image of Sandra smiling, then she saw her eyes narrowing in that canny way she had. She heard her singing and laughing, saw her dancing, heard her key in the door. Sandra. There she was kicking the pavement as she walked, too smart for them, too smart for harm. Bev hung her head and held Julie's hand, she was crying. Sandra's mother and father stood rigidly, dressed in black, as the heavy clods of earth fell onto the coffin. They couldn't share their pain with the two young strangers on the other side of the grave. Julie and Bev turned away and walked through the graveyard. The wind was blowing in the trees. Sandra had always loved wild, wet, windy days.

Waltzer

Cassie laced up her sneakers and pushed her hair out of her eyes. Her rucksack bulged beside her. As I watched her from the other side of the room, I felt paralyzed by grief. She had always said she'd go away when she was eighteen. She glanced at the clock. She'd be gone as soon as Dave arrived. She smiled her amazing big smile and chucked me a piece of gum. She chewed a lot.

We grew up together, me and Cassie. She lives in the same street as me, and we are cousins. Her family were noisy and explosive but happy. I loved going there because in my house everything was normal and voices were never raised either in anger or joy. Disputes were quelled with a look from one of my parents. We got on well enough, but there were no storms. In Cassie's house huge storms would break, followed by huge reconciliations. Sometimes my father would shake his head and say Tom and Mary, Cassie's parents, had never grown up and in time they'd realize that their children needed more discipline. There'd be trouble, mark his words; no good would come of living like that. I never said anything because my aunt and uncle seemed to create so much happiness regardless of poverty or disaster. There were others in the street who feared and disapproved of Cassie's family. One woman spent many years with her long nose poking through the net curtains fuelling her prejudices as Cassie, her brothers, sisters and parents gave her ample cause.

'Christ! Nearly forgot!' Cassie got up and stretched into a cupboard. She got out a box of chewing gum. 'Might not be able to get this where we're going.' She crammed some empty exercize books into the rucksack and smiled at me. 'We'll keep on with the diaries, OK? I'll send these back when they're full.'

We'd been keeping the diaries since we were ten. We kept them secret, and in them we told each other everything. They were dated and numbered, battered and earmarked because we'd concealed them for so long, sometimes up our jumpers or down our beds.

'Ah, one last thing. I think there's room for these – better be.' She pulled several packets of sheaths out of her back pocket. 'They might not sell these in Tibet.' She laughed.

A horn sounded outside. Dave had arrived in the van. Cassie's family went out to greet him. She looked at me. My lip was trembling. I followed Cassie as she walked down the garden path, the rucksack on her back. She grinned at everyone. Her family stood around her in a noisy untidy gaggle, kissing and tugging at her. Dave leaned on his van. He had polished it until you could see yourself quite clearly, a deformed image on the side of the door, or a huge nose in the bright chrome bumper. He leant over and polished away one last smudge with his cuff. Cassie's dad, my uncle Tom, went over to him. He put his arm around Dave's shoulders. Tom wasn't the kind to do the 'I've just one thing to say to you my son' speech. He just said 'Look after our Cass, won't you?' Dave nodded and smiled.

My dad muttered, 'Huh, that's a good one, as if anyone could look after a wild horse!'

I said 'Oh Dad!' hoping that nobody had heard him.

My mother's lips were a little too tight. She didn't approve of eighteen-year-olds running off into the blue with 'some young man' who she said 'was little better than a gipsy'. Cassie flashed my parents one of her smiles, smiles which could melt ice caps and tilt the natural order of things. My mum put her arms round Cassie and cried. That did it, everyone started crying. I hung back; it was the most unbearable moment of my life. Cassie was the wild glory I'd never be. I was the swot, the quiet one, the bookworm, but we'd shared all our thoughts all our lives and it was as though someone was taking away my arm, my leg or half of my mind. I leaned against the wall by the honeysuckle.

Cassie hugged everyone and then noticed me. She called out my name, 'Fran!' and when she saw how much I was crying she came over and put her arms round me. 'Hey, don't cry.' I sobbed. 'C'mon frog eyes, purple nose, old rubber lips, pack it in, give us a break, if you don't stop I'll start.' I shook with sobs. 'Want a piece of gum? Want a smack in the mush? Kick in the shins? A fiver? Don't cry!' And because I got worse she started too. We clung onto each other and somehow got over to the van, me, her and the rucksack. I noticed Dave sort of rolling his eyes to the sky a bit. He took the rucksack and said, 'Come on Cass, let's go.' We stood in a line waving as the van coughed its way along the street.

I went to my room feeling abandoned and forlorn. I'd always known she would leave, that the only place that could satisfy her curiosity and lust for adventure was the world out there. I had found a whole world in books but Cassie preferred to go out into the world. Most books bored her. She'd read and then fret that something was happening and she might miss it. I lay on my bed and drifted into a long reverie of memories about her and me. After a while I got out her diaries, and I lay across my bed reading them. The first book began in 1978. The writing made me laugh, it was Cassie's best joined-up writing and full of spelling mistakes:

January 10th 1978
This diary belongs to Cassie Brooks. I live at 29 Cleaver
Street, London, England, The World, The Universe.
My cousin is my best friend; her name is Fran. Her
father and my father are brothers. This [there was an
arrow pointing to a brown smudge] is Fran's and my
blood we did it with a needle now we're blood sisters.
[I remember the solemn way she announced this having
made me prick my finger against my will. Cassie was in
her manic religious phase at the time.] Marcia Lewis is
very small, that's not her fault. Me and Fran went to
church with her at 7 o'clock on Sunday. A lady got me by
the arm and said 'you didn't oughter let the little girl on
her own like that naughty girl', and I said, 'She's a
midget' and the old bag said she'd give me a good hiding
right there on the zebra crossing.

The last bit on the page made me laugh. My mother had
banned HP sauce, ketchup and salad cream. She had said
they were unhealthy. The last thing she wrote that day was
'Took Fran some salad cream, and she ate it all with her
finger in the jar and turned it upside down to get the last
bit out.'
I read on. There was the day she dared me to go to
London zoo by shinning down the side of a bridge over the
canal nearby and stalking along under high grass by the
bank and then climbing over the fence:

July 16th 1978
Fran said what if we get caught. I said act like you're deaf
and dumb. When they caught us I went 'Mmmmmm
Mmmmmm', but Fran just stood there so I pinched her
to make her cry and they left us alone. I looked at the
tigers and lions with my face against the glass. They
looked sad. The elephants heads were wagging and their

trunks were in the dust. The hippo smelled of boiled
cabbage and farts and had no room to swim. It was sad.

When we got out of the zoo Cassie kicked an empty Coke
can along the streets all the way home. She didn't say
anything. The next day she writes again:

July 17th 1978
Dad was glad me and Fran played in the street today and
didn't go anywhere. All the snakes escaped from the pet
shop in Camden Town, I wished all the animals would
escape from the zoo.

I turned the pages, seeing her at every turn, hearing her
laugh, catching a glimpse of this expression or that. I
was in all the diaries, like her shadow or her anchor,
perhaps like some cold Northern star by which she mea-
sured her experiences.

September 20th 1979
Tomorrow is Fran's birthday and she'll be eleven. We
looked at our chests in the bathroom mirror, and Fran's
got buds but I haven't. I called her Buds, but after a
while she cried. I felt guilty so I gave her Samson.

I remembered her coming round carrying something
wrapped in a tea towel, something that moved and smelled
funny. She stood at the back door and smiled showing her
two broken front teeth, smashed during a bicycle race. She
said, 'Sorry about calling you Buds, here's Samson for you.'
Samson, a rat, was her prize possession. She'd saved him
from the labs at school, stolen him. She'd kept him hidden
in an old bread-bin with holes in the garden shed. In
Cassie's terms, there was no more generous present she
could have given me.

I developed faster than Cass. She looked like a boy and

kept the wild ruthlessness and innocence of a child, but had finely tuned senses, was sensitive and intuitive. On her twelfth birthday she wrote:

October 10th 1980
I am 12 and at last I have buds like Fran's only mine are still smaller. Also hairs on my fanny; me and Fran call them forests. When we did 'Tiger Tiger Burning Bright in the Forest of the Night', Fran and me got sent out for laughing and not saying why. When I went to the toilet I found a red stain on my knickers. Mum told me and Fran about periods when we were eleven. I told Fran I'd got my period, and she said, 'Now we're women.'

Cass said 'I'm on,' because that's what we'd heard older girls saying. Somehow it got round our class and one of the boys came up to her in the playground and said 'On the rags are you?' Cassie didn't understand and asked him what he meant. He sniggered and said, 'Jam rags.'

Cassie pulled a face and said 'UGH!' and would have walked away but the boy pestered her. When the bell went he was still going on about it.

The next day I was at school before Cass because she had to go to the dentist. She came into class late, and everyone held their breath trying not to gasp and laugh. Cassie was wearing a tampon soaked in bright pink ink dangling from one ear. As she walked past the boy who had harassed her the day before, she flicked it. Luckily for her it was Miss Railton's class. She ignored the tampon and went on with the lesson. At the end she invited Cassie to explain why she was wearing the tampon. Cassie could be very polite and co-operative if a teacher deserved it. 'Thank you Miss, I'm wearing it because this kid kept going on about jam rags.' Then she went red and sat down.

'I see, well, stay behind and we'll have a chat.'

Miss Railton understood us, but most other teachers didn't even try. The headmistress Miss Haggerston hated Cassie. Miss Haggerston had the grimmest face I've ever seen, rocky and pouchy with a jagged crimson line where her mouth was supposed to be. She had mean little eyes and no trace of warmth. Another who hated Cass was Mr Creighton, the Biology teacher.

January 20th 1981
In the Biology lesson Mr Creighton asked us if we knew what had happened to his missing rat. Two years later and he's still going on about it. I hate him; he smells and his breath stinks. We call him Dog Breath. He's mean, he puts kids down and he's sarcastic. He's always getting at John Decker. He says he's thick. John Decker is scared of everyone. He stammers. Mr Creighton called him a 'big thick twit' and John Decker went red. His ears stick out and they're red and he's got freckles. Everyone teases him. 'When you are awake John Decker, perhaps you'd give the class the benefit of your wisdom,' he said. I can't stand the way teachers talk like that, really sarcastic. They seem to think it's clever and funny. We all went quiet. I put my hand up. Dog Breath said, 'Yes Cassie Brooks, I suppose that we're to get the benefit of yours instead are we?'

I said 'Why don't you pick on someone your own size?' I wanted to say why didn't he pick his nose instead but I didn't dare. He put me in detention after school for the rest of the week and made me do an essay on amoebas.

After that it was war between Cassie and Dog Breath. All it needed for actual combat was one last straw:

March 3rd 1981
Dog Breath caned two first-years for forgetting their

gym kit; they're in his class. Cassie's parents told her that if a kid got caned it had to be written in a special book, *The Punishment Book*.

March 5th 1981
I got up when Haggy had finished her lecture in assembly today. She said 'Sit down.' I was really scared but I said, 'I think it's wrong to beat kids, specially first-years, just for forgetting their PE kit.' Nobody said anything and I went really red. Some kids giggled and they all looked at me. Miss Haggerston went purple. I swear Miss Railton smiled and Dog Breath saw and his mouth screwed up. Miss Haggerston took me away and she barked at me for hours and said I was suspended and told me to go and get my coat and go home. In class everyone looked at me and nobody said anything. I felt like the only person in the world who didn't have a friend. I began to think I'd been wrong.

I remember the expression on Cassie's face as she looked round the class. Nearly betrayed, defiant, about to cry. Even Miss Railton didn't know what to say. Cassie didn't even look at me as she passed my desk. She was almost at the door and I was torn apart trying to find the courage to say something. It's probably the only time in my life that I've taken the initiative like that but my friendship and bond with Cassie were at stake. I said 'No!' very loudly. They all looked at me.

Then John Decker got up and he said 'N-n-n-n-n-n-n-no!!!' and then they all joined in and everyone said 'No'. Miss Railton looked on as though she couldn't control us and we left our desks and ran along the corridors with Cassie in the middle chanting 'No No No' until we got to Miss Haggerston's room. Cassie was unsuspended but had to apologize publicly. She did that with her hands behind her back and her fingers crossed. Her parents were called up to the school. Cassie wrote:

March 7th 1981
Mum and Dad and Fran and her parents and me sat around our kitchen table. Dad said Haggy told them 'Your daughter is a rebel and rebels come to no good in this world, she needs discipline and punishment.' Mum smiled at me and told me Haggy had said, 'I suggest you withdraw her pocket money and keep her in every weekend until she understands how to behave in a civilized manner.' Mum said it would be easier to stop a volcano erupting than keeping me in at weekends and she laughed. Fran's mum looked a bit uptight. She said, 'Well, Mary, maybe Cassie is a bit on the wild side', and Fran's Dad must have kicked her under the table because she said 'She only means to help' as Mum and Dad gave them a dirty look. My mum said 'My Cassie doesn't need taming', and my dad said 'I'd sooner tame a tiger', and that was the end of that.

I flicked on through. We were growing up. I had already had my first boyfriend and knew about kissing and what the kids at school called 'petting' although it always made me think of patting dogs. Cassie's first date affected her a lot, it made her really wary of boys for a long time.

November 5th 1982
My first date.

I smiled remembering the panic and hysterics. Cassie always wore jeans and sneakers when she wasn't at school but she wanted to look sophisticated. She went through everyone's cupboards, even my mum's, and her clothes are strictly dowdy. Cassie's first date was with this pen pal called Derek from Bournemouth. It was a blind date.

They'd been writing long letters for six months. Cassie always showed them to me and got me to check hers out. They'd never exchanged photos for some reason. But Cassie had built up a fantasy image of Derek and she wouldn't hear a word against him. I thought he sounded really full of himself and pompous, but she was blinded. The day before the date she got a little parcel. 'Oh no Fran! He's sent me a piece of his sister's wedding cake, he says 'it's to fatten me up, oh no!' Cassie wasn't exactly fat but she had become rather plump. She ate loads of sweets and usually had her hand in a packet of crisps or her mouth full of toffees. The diary went on:

> Fireworks night and I'm fourteen and going on my first date. I am wearing Fran's short black skirt which is too tight but at least it's fashionable. Fran said I should also borrow her little lace-up ankle boots, and they look OK but I'd give anything to have thin legs like Fran's. She put my eye makeup on for me and some blusher.

I laughed when I read this remembering Cassie taking her mother's best high-heeled shoes and walking up and down the street in them clacking and dragging. She was four at the time. She goes on:

> I'm feeling nervous. Suppose he wants to hold my hand and my palms are sweaty? Suppose he wants to kiss me? I've never kissed before. Fran says you press your lips together until you feel him poking his tongue between them and then you open your lips very slowly to let his tongue in but don't put your tongue in yet because he'll think you're fast. Fran has been going out with this kid Martin Lewis and they kiss quite a lot.

Cassie returned from the blind date ashen-faced. She was

speechless with misery. She concealed the diary from me
for a while but eventually she let me read it:

November 6th 1982
I ate the cake and went to meet Derek. He was standing
under the clock at Waterloo Station and I was late so he
kept looking at his watch. I thought it was funny him
looking at his watch when he was standing right under a
clock. I'd spent a few minutes hiding behind a magazine
so I could see what he was like. He was good-looking and
very smartly dressed. I'm not pretty and wondered how
I could even walk across to him. I wanted to run so I'd
get there before he could see me. I thought of my mum
saying it's not what you look like that counts. She says it's
your spirit that is important but I'm not sure what she
means because it makes me think of ghosts and whisky;
you know, the Holy Ghost and No Spirits.

Derek tried to smile when he saw me but I could see
the disappointment in his face. He said, 'Oh, I thought
you were blond' and I felt terrible. 'And for some reason
I thought you had long hair,' he went on. I cracked a joke
about having it made into a cushion for Samson, my pet
rat, the pet rat I'd given to my cousin Fran, my best
friend, I kept talking as we stood there under the clock.
He didn't seem interested. He told me what 'O' levels
he was doing, ten in all. He wasn't at all like in his
letters. He said 'Do you do any sport?' We were walking
along by then. I said I did gym at school and sometimes
me and Fran went on bike rides. He said, 'It would do
you good you know – jogging's very good for losing
weight,' and I began to hate him but I also thought
maybe he's right. Who'd want to be seen with a fat girl
like me?

He took me to MacDonald's, I love hamburgers,

especially double cheeseburgers and chips with chocolate milkshakes. As we walked in, several people looked at Derek because he's tall and good looking and I hoped they envied me. But I think they just thought what's a nice-looking guy like him doing with that frump? He asked me what I'd like to eat and I said 'Oh nothing' and I sipped a black coffee which I hate because I usually have it white with three sugars. He told me he was saving for a car and wanted a BMW but also VW Golfs had good 'performance'. I don't know a thing about cars and I'm not even interested in them but I made an effort to seem like it was all very fascinating because if you don't do that with boys they go off you really fast Fran says. I didn't say much because he didn't ask me much. But he did ask me about what kind of career I would follow. I was about to say, having thought for a minute, that I wanted to be an adventurer, but he didn't wait for my reply. He said, 'I'm going into computer design because it's a very open market.' He talked about it for ages, and I smiled and nodded and kept reminding myself about the letters and what I'd imagined he'd be like.

We went to a film and he said I could choose if I wanted. This film called *Raiders of the Lost Ark* was on, so I pretended I'd never seen it before and we went to that. It's my favourite film. He shifted in his seat all the time to show how bored he was and said 'didn't I find it all rather juvenile,' so I sort of mumbled because he said it just at the bit when the girl starts throwing glasses at the wall in a bar in Tibet because she's outdrinking the men.

I said 'Isn't she great!!' and he tried to hold my hand but it was so sweaty he soon let go. Then just as the girl flung the last glass at the wall and Harrison Ford was about to appear (I really love Harrison Ford), I said 'Isn't she great' again and Derek tried to kiss me all at the same time. I thought I shouldn't stop him although I tried to see the film over his shoulder, but then I reminded myself that this was the great moment, my first kiss! It wasn't magic at all; he stuck his tongue *straight* in my mouth and moved it round, it felt like a great wet whale. And then he tried to put his hands up my jumper, and I was really embarrassed. Even though it was only as afternoon showing there were other people in the cinema.

I struggled to my feet saying I was hungry. I thought if I had some popcorn he wouldn't try again but when I got back and had just crammed lots of it into my mouth, he started again and that did it. I started to cough and then to choke, and I mean choke, the real thing, purple in the face and spluttering bits of half-chewed popcorn everywhere. Outside the cinema he said goodbye very kind of cool, and I felt terrible when I got home. I didn't even want to tell Fran. I felt like a failure.

It was funny the way Cassie who was so outspoken and direct, so easily lost her confidence over Derek who was after all such a creep.

There was a serious fearful side to Cass. She had these dreams right from when she was a little girl, nightmares about war:

January 31st 1984
Those dreams again, New Year's Eve. Fran and me lying in a field in summer, full of wild flowers. We were talking and giggling and she was pulling bits of straw out of my hair. Then she said 'Look', and these luminous banana-shaped missiles soared soundlessly through the sky which had gone dark behind them, the colour of

blackberries. Fran cried and I put my arms round her.
The missiles were a funny colour – somewhere between
the moon and gold. We had had a debate at school about
nuclear weapons, and Fran and me were on the side that
said there shouldn't be any and others said they
prevented war, amongst them Miss Haggerston.

It wasn't long after that that Cassie made me go to school
very early and take pictures with my dad's instamatic of
things she painted on the school walls with red spray paint.
She made a real mess of the walls writing 'Nukes Out'.
Then she hid behind this tree with me and made me take
pictures of Miss Haggerston looking at her slogans in mute
helpless rage. Cassie sent them anonymously to the local
paper but they cut Miss Haggerston out of the pictures.

I turned the pages of the diaries, going backward and
forward over our years together. When she was sixteen
Cassie left school. She said there was no future in it,
she'd learned more outside. I stayed on to do 'A' levels
and she went out to work, her first job was in a pea can-
ning factory. You only have to go to the corner shop with
Cass and something will happen, she'll make an enemy
or a friend or find a lost dog or a treasure in a skip or a
dustbin.

August 20th 1984
Perhaps I should have stayed at school. I hate the pea
factory. I stand by a conveyor belt all day long picking
out blighted peas. I get £32 a week and I'm going nuts.
The supervisor says 'Our customers trust us to provide
the perfect pea and we must all take pride in the
product.' He's an oily little creep. I've been there for
three and a half weeks and today I lost my temper with
it. It was too hot to work. I said it was too hot to carry
on and he said we went on working or we were sacked.

He'd have no trouble finding other girls to work there.
We went on working.

The machines make a horrible noise all the time. He
turned up the pop music to stop us talking over the din of
the machinery so we couldn't even yell to each other.
Then the hooter went for tea break. I said to a couple of
the others that I didn't think it was right working in that
heat and that someone would pass out sooner or later.
They agreed but said there was nothing you could do,
you had to earn a living. I said we could refuse to work
until they did something about it. One of the tougher,
older women came over and said, 'We don't want any
student trouble-makers here,' and gave me a heavy look.
But another one said, 'I think Cassie's right,' and others
stood there with their arms folded nodding their heads.

There were about two-thirds of us who decided to go
back and just sit on the floor by the conveyor belt until
they did something about the heat. The supervisor
turned on the machinery and the music and I sat down on
the floor and then a couple more sat down until almost all
of us were sitting except the old battleaxe and a few who
were too scared. The supervisor turned off the machines
and the music and stood on a chair. 'You get back to work
in five minutes or you're sacked.' He was very angry. He
pointed at me, 'It's your doing isn't it? We don't want
subversives. We've never had trade unions or trouble
here.' I didn't reply because I wasn't sure what he was
talking about and didn't know what to say.

He went away and everyone started talking and
arguing, some were still for sitting in the floor but others
were losing their bottle. Then the supervisor came back
with a man in a dark blue suit with an all year suntan.

'Now then, what seems to be the matter?' he said
all smooth and polite. Nobody said anything but they

all looked at me.

'It's too hot to work,' I said a bit timidly.

Without looking at me he said, 'Carstairs, did you take this girl on?'

Carstairs mumbled and went red and admitted that he had. 'Yes sir, but . . .'

'Sir' wasn't interested in his buts and interrupted him, 'Well sack her immediately.'

That time I lost.

Cassie's childish pranks and mild delinquent ways had turned into something more serious. She thought hard and long, was changeable and moody. The diaries show that she became more inward looking:

March 27th 1985
I wish I wasn't so ugly because I'd like to have a
boyfriend now. I walk sideways-on like Egyptians in old
paintings so that there will be less of me approaching
people. Well, boys anyway, and men. I feel awkward if I
fancy them, but only because I'm ugly.

But Cassie had a natural way about her, was naturally flirtatious which made some girls jealous. Cassie didn't do it consciously but she had such immediate responses to people, was always open and curious, unless as she wrote in the diary, she fancied them. Then she was overcome with shyness which was interpreted as aggression or sullenness; she scowled. With all other boys or men she was never shy, coy or nervous. She returned a gaze or a smile and the boys we knew respected her and treated her as an equal as though in some indefinable way she exacted that from them instinctively. But after Derek she had no more boyfriends.

Even though I was the plain quiet one, I had quite a few

boyfriends. It was funny, I'd have thought it would be the other way round, that wild sassy Cassie would be the one with an exciting adventurous love-life while I swotted and was the wallflower and the gooseberry, but in situations where anyone was wallflower or gooseberry, it was Cassie, not me. Until Dave.

May 1st 1986
I was restless and it was sunny today. I got on a bus to Hampstead Heath. I'd heard there was a fair on. I wandered around feeling happy, had a go at duck-shooting, didn't win a goldfish, wondered what Fran was doing at school. Then I stood by the waltzers and watched them whirl. I wanted a ride on them so as soon as they stopped I got onto one and crammed myself into a corner waiting for the crazy motion to begin. Then this guy came over swinging from one little car to the next. There was music playing, one of my all time favourites, Annie Lennox singing 'Every-body's looking for something . . . Sweet Dreams are made of this . . .' The guy swung towards my car and leaning over, asked me casually if I was strapped in. I nodded and then the waltzers began. They lurched and rocked and crashed and I screamed and felt very excited. When I got off I was giddy and leaned against a pillar. I watched the guy swinging from car to car. He was the first boy I've ever wanted, really wanted. I can't say what it was, something about him, he was so easy with the world.

This was Dave. Cassie was very quiet that night. I was at her house having tea. I have spent most of my teens there. Her dad asked her what was up and she didn't reply. Later she told me. 'Oh Fran, I've seen this guy, he's wonderful, he's about twenty-one. What shall I do?' She didn't need to be told what to do:

May 2nd 1986
I went back to the fair and when I got there it was nearly
all packed up. The waltzers were down and I panicked
thinking maybe he wasn't there. I scanned the scene
around me, people calling out to each other about ropes
and trucks and caravans. Time passed and I sat under a
tree feeling really sad. 'What's wrong?' someone said
and slid down the tree resting on his haunches. 'Want
some gum?' he said and grinned.

Like me he had broken front teeth and before I could
stop myself I said, 'Like me, your teeth' and showed him
mine lifting my top lip to show him better.

Dave and Cassie were soon very close. They were alike –
driven by curiosity: adventurers, risk takers.

June 14th 1986
Dave says he has nine lives, I say I have nine lives. Dave
says between us we have eighteen and if we had a van
and £500 we could travel. He says he's always wanted to
go to Tibet. It suits me. I told him about the girl in the
film throwing the glasses at the wall and he didn't
interrupt or laugh. He knew what I meant and he
smiled. We're saving up, and by October we'll have
enough.

As soon as they had £500 and a van they said they were
going. I watched until the van was out of sight. I put the
diaries back tied together with a piece of red ribbon and
stowed them under my bed, as though putting our childhood away somewhere safe.

Hotel Romantika ◄

'Oh Emma! It's even better than in the brochure!'

'Yes,' Emma agreed, 'Unspoiled scenery, no discos, no Watney's, no fish and chips!'

'Bliss!' Carolyn sighed with pleasure.

'Heaven,' Emma rejoined.

'And let's hope no holiday Romeos or beach bums. English girls have a bad reputation you know.'

Carolyn was engaged to a young man she'd met at the end of the debutante season, a boy called Hugo with a lot of custardy yellow hair. Hugo and Carolyn had decided not to wait until the wedding night but kept quiet about it – nobody wanted to cause a family scandal. Until the great day both would certainly prove their devotion by remaining unquestionably faithful, not that Hugo was entirely like to do that, Carolyn thought, since a chap might feel he has a right to dally before signing his life away. A girl on the other hand, must make sure her reputation is untarnished. This was just something one had to accept. Carolyn and Emma were eighteen.

'Ohhhhh,' Emma shivered with delight. 'It really is super here.'

There was a knock at the door. A handsome dark-eyed man in waiter's uniform asked Carolyn who had opened the door, 'You like drink?'

'Ask him what they've got,' said Emma.

'What is there?' said Carolyn a little too sharply.

'Retsina, Metaxa, Ouzo, beer, orange, cock or cock flot speciality.'

'Emma, did you hear?' Carolyn gave the man a withering glance. She was sure he could pronounce Coke properly if he wanted to.

'I'll have a Coke Float,' she said. 'Emma?'

'I'll have one too – super!' (They said "cake flates" and "soopah").

'Two cake flates,' ordered Carolyn who wasn't about to say please or thank you to this uppity waiter. 'I didn't like his tone one bit,' she said turning to Emma. 'Still, it's to be expected, they're rather hot-blooded I should think.'

'I think it's awfully important that one ignore that sort of thing or they pursue one and that's frightfully tedious.'

Goldie and Tina giggled in response to the flirtatious gallantry of the Greek boys who helped them with their luggage as they boarded the tiny plane that was going to Akathos. Tina's skirt was too tight. Goldie's shirt didn't hide the pendulousness of her large breasts. She was proud of them and saw no need to disguise them. Tina was very curvy, overweight some might say, but luscious, plump and didn't give a damn about diets.

'Did you see the way he looked at you Goldie?' Goldie glanced over her shoulder as she climbed the little stairway into the plane. The two boys were smiling and waving.

'Did you see the way I looked at him?' said Goldie.

'You're a real flirt!' Tina said giggling.

'Who cares? Got to have a bit of cheek and nerve haven't you?

'Someone always cares.'

'Let them!'

As the little 'plane wobbled into the sky, they waved

through the window at the boys on the tarmac below. The 'plane toppled about in the air and Tina screamed and grabbed Goldie who laughed. There were a couple of families on the plane with them. The women were harassed by fretting children and constantly wiping dribble and melted chocolate off their faces while the men pretended they weren't trying to sneak a look at Tina's thighs or Goldie's bosoms.

'Oooh! Bloody hell! Look at that!' said Tina burying her face in Goldie's shoulder. Goldie looked down at the islands they were flying over, the mountains creased and strange, almost like models. They flew close to the cliffs and summits and Tina shut her eyes. 'I'll be sick if I look,' she said clamping her eyes shut and clutching Goldie's hand, Goldie thought it looked beautiful.

The Hotel Romantika was marble-floored, cool, white-washed. There were tall dark plants in terracotta pots behind pillars. A breeze from the sea nearby touched bright pink flowers cascading out of old earthenware urns on the terrace. Bougainvillaea hung magenta against the whiteness of the garden walls; there was red hibiscus, white oleander, frangipani, jasmin. The taxi driver who brought Tina and Goldie from the arid strip that passed for the airport, leaned against his cab, a fifties Chevrolet, and watched them gathering their profusion of possessions; they didn't travel light. He held the door as they wriggled out, tight skirts exposing white thighs, lovely girls, full of life he thought. Not like the two madams he'd brought earlier in the day. He and his cousin Iorgo drove the tiny island's two cabs.

'I am Iannis,' he said to Goldie as she struggled out of the cab. 'Plizzed to meet you.' They shook hands, Iannis wore dark glasses with mirror lenses and Goldie caught sight of herself for one approving second. Tina grinned and said she'd look forward to seeing him again.

'Plizz?'

'He doesn't understand you idiot,' said Goldie.

'Oh never mind, see you soon,' she tried again, speaking more slowly. He seemed to get the drift.

'Wasn't he gorgeous!' said Tina as the waiter led them to their rooms. He held the door open while they squeezed past, smiling and expressing their delight with the room, the balcony and the view over the orange grove. 'Goldie, this room's great,' said Tina, 'come and look at the bathroom. It's got this huge mirror and look, there's one of those things for washing your fanny!'

'Very handy,' said Goldie as she turned on their portable stereo.

Emma and Carolyn looked at each other. 'What on earth is that?' said Carolyn.

'Pop music,' Emma grimaced.

'It's ghastly! Something will have to be done.'

'I'll see the manager if it doesn't stop. It's so vulgar.'

Carolyn went out onto her balcony to see what was going on next door. Goldie was standing on the adjoining balcony swaying to the music and singing along. Carolyn pursed her lips and beckoned to Emma. As they watched, Tina emerged in an even tinier bikini than Goldie's and very dark vampy glasses. Emma and Carolyn backed into their room so they could peer at their new neighbours in an ecstasy of disgust. They heard a loud knock at Tina and Goldie's door. It was the dark-eyed waiter come to offer them a drink. Tina answered the door. She smiled. 'You like drink?'

'Yes, what is there?' Tina asked.

'Retsina, Metaxa, Ouzo, beer, orange, cock or cock flot speciality,' he said.

Goldie giggled. Tina tried to keep a straight face. 'Um, I'll have a beer please.'

'Me too,' said Goldie from inside the room.

When he'd gone they burst out laughing. 'Cock flot!' Tina said.

'Still, I suppose we'd sound pretty funny trying to speak Greek,' said Goldie.

They unpacked their clothes, far too many for ten days, but when you've saved up for as long as they had, you want to travel in style. Tina admired Goldie's wardrobe and Goldie admired Tina's. They squeezed in and out of one another's clothes and drank their beer.

'Excuse me,' said Carolyn officiously when Goldie came to the door, 'but your music is rather loud.' She stared at Goldie haughtily. 'And we came here for a quiet holiday,' she added sniffily.

'Sorry,' said Goldie. Carolyn gave her a once-over just to show her who was boss. Goldie returned the favour. 'My name's Goldie and this is Tina,' Tina peered over Goldie's shoulder suspiciously.

'My name's Carolyn and my friend's is Emma,' she said icily. It was more like an exchange of hostilities than a polite neighbourly introduction. Carolyn withdrew.

'Blimey that Chlorine or whatever her name was must have a poker up her arse,' said Goldie. They looked at each other glumly.

'I suppose that puts paid to the music,' Tina sighed.

'Just as well we brought our Walkmans,' said Goldie, 'and anyway who cares?'

The beach near the hotel was pretty but it was windy and not much good for swimming. Emma and Carolyn walked quite a long way and lay in the lee of an old boat, but the sand still whipped against them. Tina and Goldie got to the beach late. It must have been five o'clock. They swung along happily, plugged into their Walkmans, Tina singing along, well out of tune. They dumped their towels, unplugged their headsets and ran for the shoreline whooping and splashing straight into the surf.

'God, what an exhibition,' Carolyn commented.

'She's so fat!' said Emma caressing tanning oil into her perfect, smooth legs.

'Which one? Oh the short one, yes she is, I'm surprised she even goes on the beach.' She sniggered.

'Oh had enough already have they? My God, look at the way that one wobbles! it's obscene!' Tina and Goldie laughed and shook the water out of their hair. They walked up to where they'd left their towels and Tina nearly fell over scratching her leg.

'I suppose they've got fleas as well,' said Carolyn. Tina and Goldie weren't very far away and Carolyn dropped her voice. 'Look at that, she doesn't even shave her legs!' Goldie never had, the hair was blond and even it it hadn't been she wouldn't have cared.

'It's worse, she obviously doesn't give a damn about the bikini line either! Do you suppose they're women's lib or something? I wouldn't have thought so, but honestly!' Tina was rubbing Goldie's back with a towel, Goldie laughed and Tina tickled her and they struggled and toppled over in the sand. 'It's disgusting,' said Carolyn and turned over. Emma stared on.

'Do you think there'll be any nice single men in the hotel?' said Tina.

'Well, didn't look too hopeful at first glance did it? Small hotel too isn't it? said Goldie.

'Oh I don't mind, it makes a change after that resort we went to last year in Spain.

'Yes, after that I fancied this, nice and quiet.' Goldie smiled.

'We'll have to case the joint at dinner, see what the talent is.'

The dining room was open-plan and led onto the terrace. The nights were hot and big old-fashioned fans whirred softly over the guests' heads. Tina and Goldie had put on nice dresses and makeup but their spirits sank when they saw who else was in the dining room. 'Families, all families,' said Tina sadly.

'Oh well, never mind, maybe there'll be some fun somewhere else.'

'And men aren't everything,' Tina sighed.

'We can read our books and write letters, we'll do really well in the evening class this year. We could always read Wuthering Heights and get ahead.'

'Ugh!' Tina groaned.

'Oh Tina, it's dead romantic really once you get into it!' she paused reflectively, 'but I know what you mean, I like a bit of real romance on holiday.'

Emma and Carolyn sat a couple of tables away. They were clean and well groomed, wearing the kind of expensive clothes that subtly ooze style and never crease. Goldie strained her ear to catch what the other girls were saying. Their conversation revolved around births, marriages, deaths, christenings, cocktails, balls, weekends in the country and two men called Hugo and Jamie. There seemed to be a never-ending supply of major occasions for them to absorb themselves in and Goldie imagined she was seeing snapshots of all these festivities. They talked about what everyone wore, even to funerals. Goldie had always assumed everyone wore black and that was that and she thought it was horrible to talk about funerals in the same way as weddings, all a matter of fashion and who did and didn't get snubbed.

Tina nudged Goldie, 'Cheer up, come on let's go outside and have a brandy on the terrace.'

When the waiter brought their brandy he said, 'You nice girls, you like another bitch?' This restored their good spirits and made them laugh. The waiter laughed too and Tina thought how nice his smile was. 'I know very nice bitch, my cousin Iannis, he has taxi, he take you to nice bitch, beautiful.'

'What's your name?' Tina asked the waiter.

'I am Stavros,' he said. They all smiled.

Emma and Carolyn had overheard this conversation. 'Hmm, I'd like to see his other beach wouldn't you Emma?' said Carolyn.

'Yah, I would.'

'I don't know that I could bear to share a taxi with those two, but a nice sheltered beach would make all the difference wouldn't it?'

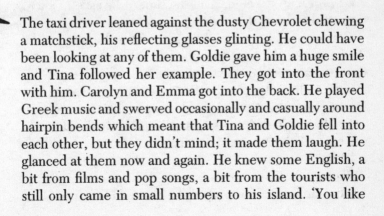

The taxi driver leaned against the dusty Chevrolet chewing a matchstick, his reflecting glasses glinting. He could have been looking at any of them. Goldie gave him a huge smile and Tina followed her example. They got into the front with him. Carolyn and Emma got into the back. He played Greek music and swerved occasionally and casually around hairpin bends which meant that Tina and Goldie fell into each other, but they didn't mind; it made them laugh. He glanced at them now and again. He knew some English, a bit from films and pop songs, a bit from the tourists who still only came in small numbers to his island. 'You like

Greece?' he asked.

'Yes yes,' said his two front passengers.

'Greece good, orea, beautiful, kalo,' he said.

'Hey, you teach us a Greek word, we'll teach you an English one, OK?'

'En daxi, en daxi, OK!' he replied enthusiastically.

'You like England?'

'Feefty feefty America. Beezy beezy, work bad. Akathos doulia, work –'

'Doulia means work?' said Goldie.

'Ne, yes, poli doulia, much work America. Akathos doulia Junio, Julio, Avgost, Septiembro, Oktomber – feenis. Fishing, no problema.' Goldie thought of the office all year, too much work, poli doulia. Fishing no problema she thought.

They swung onto a rocky track high above a sheltered cove and wound down the track. He stopped at a cafe with a roof made of bamboo. The taxi driver pointed to his watch, six o'clock, he'd come back for them. En daxi. Goldie wondered exactly what en daxi meant assuming it had something to do with taxis but then why did everyone keep saying it? Maybe they were all obsessed with taxis. 'Why does everyone say en daxi all the time?' she asked Tina as they strolled towards a beautiful sandy cove.

Carolyn and Emma walked away from the other girls. 'Did you see the way they flirted with that taxi driver!' Carolyn said. 'Especially the one with the hairy legs, God, it really is disgusting.' Secretly Emma found the taxi driver exciting and attractive but she'd never admit it to Carolyn.

Goldie and Tina spread out their towels and lay down to sun bathe. 'Oh Tina, isn't he gorgeous!'

'Who?'

'Yanny.'

'It's I–anni not Yanny, you make it sound like nanny.'

'So handsome, like a French film star. I once saw this film with subtitles but I couldn't be bothered to read them because there was this wonderful guy with dark glasses. I think he was a gun-runner and at the end he tied these sticks of dynamite round his head and just blew himself up. He said "Oh merde", (that means Shit!). He had this girl-friend that murdered a fat man in a bath with a pair of nail scissors. Yanny looks like the film star – the gun-runner.' After that they often referred to Ianni as the gun-runner. Goldie lay back and thought of romance.

At lunchtime the few people in the cove and secluded beaches nearby, drifted into the taverna and sat under the bamboo roof eating lunch. By the time Tina and Goldie got there all the tables were occupied, they shared one with a stern looking man, a good deal older than them.

'Do you mind if we –'

'Pliss to sit down.' He was German and was reading an enormous book.

'What are you having Tina?'

'Chips and beer and salad.'

Carolyn and Emma were two tables away. 'The fat one's having chips, honestly, it's amazing!' Carolyn said. Emma glanced at her, she was getting irritated by her friend's preoccupation with these two girls. Emma looked round. She had noticed the German before. There was something intriguing about him. He struck a contrast to the angular Englishmen from the Hotel Romantika who discussed property and shares and transport with each other.

'I think I'll have fish,' said Goldie.

'Yes! Fish straight from the sea, let's have that,' Tina said.

The German turned the pages of his book without look-ing up. His dinner arrived. Fish. He carefully wiped the knife and fork with his napkin and set about removing the entrails. Tina looked at Goldie, stifling a laugh. Emma watched from the corner of her eye. The German looked up and caught the last flash of Goldie's smile. 'You sink is funny?' he said.

'No! I mean . . .'

'I am surgeon you know,' he said by way of explanation without a trace of humour. Tina said how interesting to meet a surgeon on holiday especially one from Germany. Their fish arrived. Goldie got in a mess trying to cut it up. 'Allow me to help you,' the surgeon offered.

'Oh don't worry, I can deal with the dorsal aortas myself thanks,' replied Goldie.

'Vimmen hev no idea,' he said with a supercilious, contemptuous smile. Goldie looked up at him frankly.

'Is that so? What about women surgeons then?'

'Impossible! Ziss is stupid! Vimmen couldn't do ziss, zey are too weak.'

'Oh come on,' said Goldie. 'Give over! We have babies don't we? Weak?' she said, 'Huh,' and went on trying to cope with the fish.

'Yah, sure, but a voman couldn't stand up for twelf hours for ze micro brain surgery.'

'Course they could! Do you know some women go through hours and hours labour before even having the baby.'

'Ach, yah, but zen zey are on sere backs vere zey belong.' Goldie wished she could think of a fast reply but her mind went blank, so she gave him what she hoped was a cutting look and got on with her lunch. 'Stupid . . . vimmen can't do brain surgery . . .' he muttered on.

'Listen, I heard we're going to outstrip men at the marathon soon you know, so we're catching up and taking over, you'd better watch out,' Goldie said and laughed because he looked so grim. Emma caught bits of this and at one point she and Goldie exchanged a look, some trace of recognition. Goldie got on with her lunch and the surgeon returned to his book. Emma watched him; she noticed that he had a harpoon lying at his feet. A hunter.

A couple of unremarkable days passed. Their tans deepened. They ate, slept, chattered, read books. Tina's longing for discos subsided, and Goldie was a little more fascinated by Iannis everyday. They had exchanged various vital phrases: 'It doesn't matter. So what? I'm very well today thank you. My mother is well too. Do you like swimming/water melon/my island? What a lovely day, good-night, no thank you.'

Meanwhile Tina was falling for Stavros, the waiter. 'Oh Goldie, I love his accent. He asked me if I'd like to see this special bay he knows, I said . . .'

'Don't tell me, you said could you bring your friend and he said sadly . . .'

'He said the boat's only big enough for two.'

'I see,' Goldie laughed.

'He said tomorrow's his day off. What do you reckon?'

'I think you're nuts if you go to a beach alone with a strange man.'

'Stavros isn't strange, he's not a stranger! I've spoken to him almost as much as you've spoken to Ianni.'

'The gun runner. . . .'

'Sssh, here comes Stavros.' They were sitting on the terrace. The cicadas were singing and there were a million stars in the Mediterranean sky. Goldie gazed up at them hoping for a shooting star so she could make a wish.

'Good evening leddies,' said Stavros. The two girls smiled, Goldie reluctantly shifting her gaze before she'd had a chance to see a falling star. 'You come to my bitch tomorrow?' said Stavros. Tina looked at Goldie, Goldie smiled and shrugged very slightly. 'I come back five meenits, you tell me,' said Stavros, moving away.

'Goldie, I really like him, he's nice.'

'You mean you fancy him, he's sexy. What's wrong with that?'

'Oh I dunno, just that nobody ever says that do they?'

'But they all think it.'

'It's just the way you're brought up I suppose. I mean if we were at home, nobody'd mind me getting to know a guy and going for a boat-ride would they?'

'I suppose not,' said Goldie thinking about it.

'And I do trust him,' Tina went on.

'Mmm. The gun-runner taught me some new words to-day: frontier, sort of, and pineapple.' Goldie laughed.

Stavros was back. 'Pliss, you come? My brother he wants to know if I use bott tomorrow.'

'I think you use bott tomorrow,' said Goldie smiling.

There were only two days left. Emma was manicuring her toe nails while Carolyn wrote cards; each one said the same thing, weather . . . food . . . wish you were here . . . super time . . . Caro . . . she stopped and looked at Emma who had begun to paint each nail very carefully with a subtle pink varnish. Should she tell her about Jonty? She thought not; she didn't want to risk tarnishing her reputation and she certainly didn't want to be like those two sluts who made it obvious with taxi drivers and waiters. Besides, this was different.

The day before, Carolyn and Emma had got up late and missed the taxi so they'd gone to the windy beach. Carolyn had gone back during the afternoon to get something. Jonty was there, reading a magazine about cars. 'Hi! Nice and cool in here isn't it?' he said as Carolyn walked by. 'Fancy a drink?' Carolyn thought why not, and sat down.

And then Jonty suddenly began to pour out his heart to her. In a sudden, uncontrollable fit of misery he told her how bored he was with his wife, that he thought he was going mad. Carolyn had noticed the wife, and thought she was awfully plain and rather fat, always worrying over the children. What a bore for a full-blooded man like Jonty. Poor man. He had to get rid of his sexual energies slamming a ball around a squash court three times a week. The wife was always too tired for sex, besides, he added it was damned difficult to be excited by a woman who had let herself go like that. Her sympathy went out to him and her blood was up. Jonty clasped her hand and breathing heavily, propositioned her – the next afternoon, her room, what a fine-looking young woman she was, he was quite overcome. Nobody had every thrown themselves like this at Carolyn and she liked it. Oh for goodness sake, she reasoned, nobody will ever know, but how to get Emma out of the way?

Emma ate her breakfast and drank her coffee. Carolyn sat with her head in her hands and said nothing. She sighed once or twice. 'You OK Caro?' asked Emma.

'Frightful headache, think I'd better stay here today.'

'I'll stay with you.'

'No, no, there's no need. I'll just lie in the dark with a damp towel over my eyes. You go to the nice beach, such a shame we missed the taxi yesterday.

'Well, are you sure though Caro?'

'Certain, please, so decent of you, but must lie down in peace.' Carolyn got up and walked slowly towards their room. Jonty and his wife and children were eating their breakfast. He watched this scene marvelling at women's ability to lie. That's the sort of man he was. Never trust a woman was his motto, and then he looked at his long-suffering wife. He tried to imagine her with another man. The accountant at the next table, the doctor three tables away? No, who'd want to go to bed with her? Besides she was a married woman, his wife and the mother of his children.

That afternoon, Jonty slipped into Carolyn's room. She gave herself to him with tremendous vigour and absolutely no trace of guilt. They didn't exchange words of love, that was not what it was about.

Goldie sat in front with the taxi driver and Emma sat behind. The taxi wove around the familiar bends. 'Today we do car,' said Iannis to Goldie. And so she learned gear-stick, rear-view mirror and steering-wheel. Emma was amused. Against her better judgement there was some-thing she liked about Goldie, but she wouldn't let it get to her. In Carolyn's absence she relaxed a little. She looked out of the window and occupied her mind with thoughts of Jamie and what it would be like if he popped the question. She'd be Lady Davenport when his mother died. She imagined the wedding, the ball, the guests . . .

'Windscreen wipers,' said Goldie waving her arms this way and that in imitation of windscreen wipers.

Emma strolled away with her towel and her book and Goldie lingered for a few minutes with the taxi driver exchanging more automobile vocabulary. 'Also I tell you beautiful words . . .'

'I'm going the day after tomorrow,' said Goldie.

'Tomorrow go?'

'No, after tomorrow.'

'En daxi, met avrio.' He looked sad. 'I see you tomorrow night?'

Goldie laughed and got out of the cab. She walked away towards the beach. There were never more than ten or twenty people and Goldie made sure she was nowhere near the surgeon whose blue moped she had noticed leaning against the cafe wall. She was surprised just how much she enjoyed the day on her own having always thought of herself as a good-time girl surrounded by people, noise, laughter. She daydreamed about the taxi driver. She imagined a little time spent with him on her last evening, romantic and a little sad.

At lunchtime Emma went to the taverna. She was ravenously hungry. Carolyn wasn't there so she decided to have a big plate of chips, a bottle of beer and an ice cream. She had only just begun to be aware of what a strong influence her friend had on her. Appearances were so important to Carolyn; even on holiday she didn't risk adding a pound or two to her perfect weight. 'You are alone today? I may join you?' The surgeon sat down. Emma smiled and got on with her chips hoping he wouldn't find her appetite unfeminine. 'It is good, you are eating ze chips, I like a voman vizz a healsy appetite.' He put his harpoon down carefully and gave Emma an appreciative look.

When Goldie arrived for her lunch she was interested to see Emma deep in conversation with the surgeon. She didn't like him one bit herself but had to admit he had a certain power and was handsome. But cold, and above all Goldie was attracted by warmth. Goldie ate her lunch and read her book.

It was almost six o'clock. Goldie was back at the bamboo-roofed taverna. The wind was restless and heavy with the oppressiveness of the Meltemi which blew from the deserts of Africa across southern Europe. It was humid, fevered. Goldie shivered, waiting beneath the rustling bamboos for the gun-runner to take them back to the Hotel Romantika. He was late. Emma was nowhere to be seen.

The sea brooded, the sky darkened.

When the taxi driver finally arrived, there was still no sign of Emma. Goldie refused to go without her and just as the wind was really beginning to whip at the sea and the trees, Emma appeared with the surgeon. 'I wonder if you wouldn't mind awfully telling Carolyn that our German friend will be giving me a lift back later on his scooter?' Goldie nodded, not taken in for a second. The wind would be howling later, any fool could see that, and the little blue scooter would never make it up that track in the dark.

But Goldie said, 'OK,' and added 'Take care.' The two girls exchanged a smile in which there was a trace of conspiracy.

The taxi growled up the track away from the increasingly stormy bay. Bazouki music wailed from the tape deck. 'Tomorrow you come we drink Greek taverna no tourist, play bazouki?' He smiled. Goldie smiled. They had spoken to each other every day for a week, communicating even if it was door handle, headlight, the sister of my mother, I like tomatoes. He had never touched her. Goldie appreciated this, she felt respected. Occasionally on a sharp bend she had involuntarily and briefly leaned against him, feeling the hair on his arms brush hers.

'Yes, all right,' she said, 'I come with you tomorrow evening.'

'Oh Goldie, I'm in love, really in love this time.'

'Yeah?'

'He took me to this cove he knows. He said he had never taken a girl there before. He said he would show me his island and I would meet his mother. We went in this little boat, he rowed. When we got there he said I was the most beautiful English girl he'd ever seen! Me! Beautiful!' She was glowing. Goldie nodded and smiled. 'He said he'd never felt this way before and that he wanted to show me how much he cares. He gave me this little locket to wear – see? And do you know what else he said? He said I was all women to him. Isn't that amazing?' She had a quick swoon and started again. 'Then he put his arms around me and Goldie, it was just like in films when they crush the girl in their arms on a beach. He kissed me then and he said he had never felt such soft lips as mine. We lay down to sunbathe. He put oil on my back. He speaks very good English, knows loads of phrases. He lay beside me and he ran his fingers up and down my back. He whispered in my ear, "Did anyone ever tell you your skin is like silk?" Well, nobody ever has so I said "No they haven't actually." He said "What fools these English men are!" He looked deep into my eyes. He said, "Your eyes are more beautiful than the stars" and then he kissed me again. Oh Goldie, and do you know what he said then? He said "I have longed for this moment." ' She paused and went all moony.

Goldie was trying not to laugh but couldn't stop herself. 'I know, don't tell me, then he said, "Tina, be mine!" '

'Goldie it's not like that, it's real!!' Tina said, looking aggrieved. But not for long, she lapsed right back into soft focus with no encouragement at all. 'He said other girls had tried to entice him, but he had never laid a hand on a tourist before. He said I was special to him. He said he would wait for me and next year we could be together again and I could stay. Oh Goldie!'

Tina couldn't eat; she stared in wonder into the distance. Goldie looked around the dining room. The red-faced sporty type who always looked as if he was about to bust out of his flesh, looked even porkier than usual. Goldie couldn't stand the sight of him. Carolyn sat with her back to Goldie and Tina reading a book. When Goldie had told her

that Emma was with their 'German friend' she had thanked
her icily. Goldie looked at the rest of the guests. Normal,
she thought. Nice, normal, safe and dull, she thought. The
women were forever wiping their children's faces. Best let
them be grubby on holiday, Goldie would have thought,
save you the trouble of spitting on endless hankies and
rubbing their unwilling little faces every five minutes. One
last sigh from Tina. 'Well,' said Goldie, 'and what then?'

'We just kissed and you know, a bit, well,' she said coyly.

'You mean you didn't . . .'

'No, course not!'

The last day came. Tina and Goldie went to meet the taxi
driver. As they walked through the courtyard, Goldie said,
'Tina, tonight after dinner I am going for a drive with the
gun-runner.'

Tina smiled. 'And I am going for a walk with the waiter,'
she said. They laughed.

Iannis was late and the two girls sat on the edge of the
terrace in the sun. Goldie shaded her eyes and looked
along the road. She saw a blue scooter draw up under a tree
just far enough away to be beyond ear shot. Emma climbed
off the pillion seat. Goldie wished she could hear what they
were saying. She caught snatches of music from the tape-
recorder the German had over the handle bars – it sounded like opera. After a couple of minutes, the German drove
off. Emma approached the hotel looking, Goldie thought, a
bit the worse for wear. Goldie was about to greet her but
their fleeting recognition might never have happened.
Emma walked past, her head held high, staring straight
ahead as if Goldie didn't exist.

The day passed tranquilly. The wind had died down, the
sea was calm and bright blue. They lay in the sun enjoying
their last day. 'Do you know what Greek for sea is?'

'No,' said Tina half asleep in the sun.

'Thalassa. Isn't that a nice word. Thalassa, thalassa,' Goldie repeated.

Tina frowned and looked at her. 'Getting a bit poetic aren't you?' she said. Goldie wanted to savour every moment of her last day before returning to the city and the dreary routine of her office job.

In the late afternoon just before Iannis came to get them, Goldie and Tina said goodbye to the old woman who ran the cafe with the bamboo roof. She gave them little glasses of milky Ouzo and salty black olives. She smiled and talked and they smiled and nodded. She pinched their cheeks affectionately. As the taxi wove around the bends on the steep track leaving dust trails in the air, Goldie looked back at the great serenity of the bay beneath already feeling nostalgic. Goldie and Tina were silent. Goldie sat in the middle watching the worry beads and the plastic icon swinging from the rear-view mirror and listening to the Greek pop music on the radio. Emma and Carolyn hadn't been with them that day. As Goldie got out of the cab at the hotel, Iannis said, 'You meet me ennea under feeg tree.' Goldie wasn't sure what ennea meant, Iannis counted out on his fingers – nine o'clock.

He sat in the Chevrolet under the fig tree. She walked into the beam of the headlights and he leaned over to open the door. He was smoking a cigarette, one arm slung along the back of the bunk seat. Goldie got into the car. He said some long words which she didn't understand. 'What?'

'Iannis say free, Iannis say love.' Occasionally he would say Iannis say something, it meant what he was saying was more serious. Goldie smiled but was a little put out by the sudden importance of his greeting. 'Five meenits car drink gasoline then drive, OK?' he said. He got out and filled the tank from a petrol container. Goldie noticed something rolling along the seat – a water melon, there were also two loaves of bread. He got back in and started the engine.

They drove along for a while. Goldie was beginning to relax and enjoy her romantic drive when he turned abruptly off the road into an orchard. He stopped. This wasn't what she had imagined it would be like. She had expected a long soothing romantic drive around the island, stopping at a taverna somewhere for a drink. They would kiss a few times. Despite her raunchy appearance and up-front manner, Goldie was a romantic and she sensed something altogether a bit practical about his moves. Trying to make things seem right, Goldie pointed to the melon and the bread. 'You eat a lot of bread!' she joked, 'And a big melon.' He smiled uncomfortably. Goldie shifted in her seat. Something dug into her back. A child's shoe. She hadn't thought whether he was married or not, and realized then that she'd assumed he wasn't. Goldie held out the little shoe. 'You got kids?' she said.

'Iannis, pedia? Ochi,' he made a very typically Greek gesture nodding his head backwards emphasizing the ochi, no. 'You pedia?' he asked Goldie.

She still had the little shoe in her hand. She shook her head, 'No, no kids yet.'

'You like free,' Iannis said, 'Iannis like free.' He showed her his hands, no rings. 'Is Iannis trianda,' he indicated three times ten with his hands held out. 'Trianda pende have keeds, now free.'

Iannis turned on the radio and got out of the car. He came round to her door and drew her out. Goldie hoped they were going to dance in the headlights, there was no moon. But that wasn't his intention. Instead he propelled her into the back seat of the car. She didn't know how to explain that this wasn't what she wanted. They sat in the back with the doors closed. He was about to kiss her when, feeling claustrophobic, Goldie opened a door. A light came on and he blinked. Goldie giggled, suddenly it was all becoming comical. She looked around the car: torn red plastic seats, dusty old dashboard, bits of paper, a comb and a crucifix stuffed above the sun shade, his hat on the floor, a baseball team name embossed in it. He shut the door and they were in the dark again, the music playing. He caressed her cheek and ran his hands through her thick wiry blond hair. Goldie realized it was too late to explain. He hadn't understood her warmth, and she couldn't think of any way to talk about how she felt. Once they stopped swapping vocabulary and exchanged concepts any weightier than windscreen wiper, they were into emotional territory that was strange and daunting to Goldie. Iannis gently pushed her onto her back and put his hand inside her shirt, Goldie realized that girls like her didn't exist in his world. They were either virgins fiercely protected by fathers and brothers, or wives, mothers or grandmothers dressed in black and bound by duty.

Iannis was saying 'I love you Goldie,' as he kissed her neck. 'You are beautiful,' he said again and again. The door sprung open again and Goldie began to see the funny side as the car bounced around and the lights went on and off and the music wailed and grew more frantic. She returned his kisses more in the spirit of complicity than with the romantic passion she had anticipated. Her bare legs were sticking to the plastic covering on the seats. She shifted and made it clear that enough was enough. She wished she knew the Greek for 'I don't want to go all the way,' feeling a bit mean as she gave him a gentle shove. He was a little embarrassed as he disentangled himself and half fell out of the car. They sat under a tree on the edge of the orchard looking at the sea.

'Thallassa, thallassa,' said Goldie, and smiled.

On the way back two men hailed the taxi. Red-faced Jonty and one of the angular Englishmen from the hotel got in. Jonty leered knowingly at Goldie who looked straight through him. At the hotel Iannis took the two men's money first and they got out and went off amidst badly suppressed guffaws. Goldie parted well with her gun-runner, kissing him on the cheek and pressing his hand warmly. As she walked across the terrace she ignored Jonty and his companion who watched her with a mixture of lust and disdain.

It was the last morning. Tina slept late. Goldie was starving and went to the dining room. The families were all there; parents saying 'Don't Simon' and 'Say please Julian,' and 'No you can't Rosemary'. Whatever they thought about Tina and Goldie, they had always been civil, saying good morning or hello or nice evening. But on the last morning they ignored Goldie. She poured herself some coffee and buttered a roll. She looked round. Most days a couple of the children had chatted with Goldie and Tina. After a little while one of red-faced Jonty's daughters came over to Goldie. She stood in front of Goldie and said, 'My daddy says he saw you with the taxi driver last night, my daddy says you are a . . .' the child said this very smugly. She had learned the ways of her parents by the age of eleven.

'He says I'm a what?' said Goldie as mildly as she could.

'He says you're bad.'

'Oh does he? Well tell your daddy this; tell him he can kiss my arse.' The child clapped her hand over her mouth and scurried back to her father. Goldie didn't wait for the debacle, she returned to her room feeling humiliated and angry with herself for losing her temper with a child, angrier still with the child's father for using his children like that.

Tina was awake staring into space. 'Goldie, he says he'll write to me every week and be waiting for me next year. I'm in love.'

'Great,' said Goldie angrily.

'What's wrong?' said Tina sitting up.

Goldie went into the bathroom and came out with her toothbrush in her mouth and the toothpaste foaming out. 'They ignored me and this little girl comes up and says "My daddy saw you with the taxi driver last night." '

'Have you looked in the mirror today?' Tina asked.

'No.'

'Well perhaps you should.' Goldie had had love bites before but this was something else. She gasped.

The little aeroplane rattled along the runway and clattered into the sky, heaving itself over the peaks of the island and out of sight. Below Stavros and Iannis watched it disappear. Tina clutched a piece of paper in her hand; she and Stavros had swapped addresses at the last minute. She was trying not to cry. Goldie was wearing a scarf and feeling really hot. Carolyn was tight-lipped; she filed her nails. Emma looked out of the window.

The Poodles of Doom

Mandy was eating a banana. There were a few people sitting round the large table, all older than her. She felt shy but was fascinated by them. Her older brother Paul had taken her there. The people were what Mandy thought of as 'arty'. Paul was talking to a much older man with a strange interesting face and short, well-cut, greying hair. They were looking at a book full of glossy reproductions and nodding significantly. Mandy didn't know what to make of the paintings. She'd done a term at art college, most of which had been spent making a reconstruction of a melon out of clay and learning to measure proportions in life class. The two men rubbed their chins and drank from tall glasses. Mandy sipped her wine and tried to look interested. 'What do you think of this?' Paul asked the man with greying hair.

He looked at it, screwing up his eyes, 'Mmmm,' he said. They both said 'Mmmm' a lot. The older man looked at Mandy, she was embarrassed and looked away. 'What do you think?' he asked her showing her the book, his expression amused.

Mandy looked at the book, bending her head so that her face would be concealed behind her long auburn hair. She didn't know what to say. They were abstract paintings and Mandy only liked paintings with shapes she could identify, otherwise it looked to her like kids could have done it, but she was reluctant to be thought immature or lacking in understanding, this after all was art. 'Dunno,' she said.

The man with the greying hair said, 'Oh come on, you must think something!'

Mandy bit into the banana and chewed. She had never been good at concealing her feelings or opinions in spite of her sudden bouts of shyness. The words would out, 'Well actually I think monkeys could have done them.' The two men laughed and turned away, back to their important discussion. Mandy folded the banana skin and put it on a plate. The wine was going to her head.

'That was unfair,' said their hostess, a wiry little woman called Julia with manic eyes. 'How should Mandy know? How old are you Mandy?' Julia was trying to be kind but Mandy wished she would shut up and leave her alone, instead of drawing attention to her and making her feel even more ignorant. 'Oh eighteen! What a lovely age,' Julia sighed. 'Wait until you're an old lady like me – thirty-eight,' she said.

Mandy didn't like to agree that it did seem very old. And the odd thing was that Julia didn't seem worked out in the way Mandy expected people of her age to be. It puzzled her that the adult world should be different to the world of childhood or adolescence, and yet she was discovering that some adults seem to feel as muddled as people of her own age.

Mandy unpeeled another banana to give herself something to do but it tasted weird mixed with the alcohol which she wasn't used to. She'd have preferred Coça Cola but didn't want to seem childish. She sipped at the sour wine, suppressing the desire to wrinkle her nose. Julia chattered on. Paul and the grey-haired man pored over the book. There wasn't much mileage to be made out of the banana and the grey-haired man was watching Mandy. She wished she'd chosen an apple instead, it would have taken longer to eat. Julia turned her attention to a woman with long brown hair and a high forehead, large clear eyes and an attentive air about her, a writer Mandy had been told. What was Mandy supposed to do in this adult world? There were some other people but they hadn't noticed her, why should they? Or perhaps they had but saw no reason to engage her in conversation. She looked at them. Their faces told stories, lines creeping around eyes and mouths. Mandy hoped Julia's unruly children would stay outside in the garden. She took a large red apple from the bowl and ate it as slowly as she could. She strolled over to the window and sat on the sill watching Julia's untamed children pulling an old bicycle to bits in the long weed-tangled grass under the over-arching branches of a knotty pear tree. She felt older than the children in the garden for whom broken bikes and bricks and rubble were enough to build a fantasy world. But nor did she feel part of the generation behind her who talked art and life.

'What are you thinking about?' It was the grey-haired man. He was carrying the book. She concentrated hard on the last bit of her apple. She didn't say anything. His presence caused a confusion like all the radio channels playing at once so that it was impossible to hear any of them properly. It was an exciting sensation but not necessarily a pleasant one. It was entirely new to her. 'Maybe you're right,' he went on. 'Perhaps monkeys could have done them.' He laughed. He seemed very much at ease beside her on the window sill. He was tall and strong. She noticed his arms and they unnerved her. Mandy glanced round. Paul was talking to Julia. 'Paul tells me you are an art student,' said the grey-haired man.

'Yes,' said Mandy.

'And what kind of art do you like?'

'Well, I like things I can recognize,' Mandy began, thinking of statues and portraits.

'So do I, my work is all of people – very straightforward.' He was watching her and she felt embarrassed. 'What are you doing with your summer holidays then?' he asked.

'I'm a waitress.' Mandy was working in a restaurant in West London, a long way from where she lived.

'Oh where? Is it fun?' he asked.

'It's OK, quite funny sometimes. It's a little place down an alley in Kensington.'

'What's it called – perhaps I know it?' She told him the name of the restaurant. He said he'd never heard of it.

It was an alarmingly hot day. Mandy sweated as she worked. In the middle of the small dark restaurant there was a group of the manager's friends. The manager was a greasy, seedy little man. Mandy served up fancy dishes to these men and one, a regular, sat back ostentatiously to make room for her. He was wearing an open-necked shirt and an expensive gold chain nestled in the hair that grew thickly on his chest. Mandy imagined that he worked at nights in a casino; he wasn't a creature of daylight. There was something dirty about him although a smell of male perfume emanated from him and he was very smoothly dressed and well-manicured. He usually hassled Mandy who didn't know how to deal with his attentions. He took hold of her arm and ran a finger along its pale inside. She had a hot plate in her other hand which made it difficult to snatch the other arm away. She bristled. His friends laughed in low lascivious enjoyment. Then he curled his lip and said, 'Sweaty!' and let her arm drop. She slammed the plate down and walked quickly away.

It was a thundery day and suddenly the rain came

pelting down. The customers from the tables outside hurried into the restaurant carrying plates and glasses. Mandy looked round for the manager and his assistant. Nowhere to be seen. A man in a corner banged a glass systematically on a table demanding another lager. Normally he would have been pacified by the manager and eased out of the door. 'You, waitress, bring me another lager!' he bellowed. Mandy gave him a dirty look. A chorus was building up; they all wanted their bills, more food, tables, somewhere to dry out after the lashing rain, their second course, more coffee. Mandy cursed the manager and his assistant – everyone knew they were having an affair, but what a time to disappear. She turned to the young man behind the bar for help.

He smiled at her absolutely vacantly showing a row of gappy teeth. 'Sorry,' he said, he was drunk and working so slowly that he was less than useless.

The chefs. Mandy decided, she'd ask them to help. They worked in the basement. She ran down the stairs; it was horribly hot and there was an overpowering smell of garlic and hot fat. The two chefs looked round as she appeared. They were having a row. Mandy ran back up the stairs. The till jammed as she tried to cope with the bills, and the customers' complaints and demands increased from a rumble to a roar; above the din the drunk howled for another beer and swearing. Outside the rain came down like Bible weather.

And then Mandy did a wonderful thing. She stood in the middle of the restaurant and she yelled 'Shut up shut up shut up!!!!' and they did, stunned, all except for the drunk who went on banging on the table and howling for beer. Outside thunder crashed and lightning split the sky. Mandy was amazed and delighted by her boldness but not at all sure what to do next. The customers began to mutter restlessly.

It was at this point that the grey-haired man appeared in the doorway dripping wet. He took in what was happening and began to laugh. Mandy looked up and saw him. He walked straight over to her and took her by the hand. 'Come on, let's go,' he said. Mandy looked round at the customers who were muttering amongst themselves, the lager drinker endlessly beating out his demands on the table. And then she turned to the man 'Yes,' she said recklessly, 'let's!'

They ran down the alleyway in the rain and Mandy yelled, 'Hey, what's your name?'

'Bob Lomax,' he shouted back at her as he slipped the key into the passenger door of a car. Mandy fell gladly into his old Jaguar. It had real leather seats and a walnut dashboard. She was excited, she was on an adventure, like a child who despite all she's learned about strange men and sweets still thinks it's all right to talk to them sometimes and anyway feels herself to be beyond harm. Mandy couldn't believe that anyone meant to hurt her. She hadn't learned to be suspicious. The adult world beckoned and she followed, fascinated. She looked sidelong at Bob Lomax as he weaved in and out of the traffic. She wondered how old he was – thirty-five – forty? He was handsome in an ordinary sort of way she thought but practically old enough to be her father. She wondered why he had come to see her and was flattered. Some new strange thrill stirred within her.

'I was just passing,' he said. Mandy believed him, why shouldn't she? The radio played on a pop station and they didn't speak for a while. 'Here we are,' he said as he parked in front of a small terraced house. They ran to the door. He turned the key. 'Henry! Henry! Henry!' he called out in a strange high-pitched tone. Two closely clipped poodles scuttled down the uncarpeted stairway, their claws clattering. They wagged and sniffed and jumped up and down, barking and yelping. Mandy backed off, how come they were all clipped so close to their skin? There was something weird about it. He patted and stroked them and let them lick his face. Mandy could never understand how people could let dogs do that thinking about the ways dogs greeted each other when they met in the street. 'They're both called Henry,' Bob Lomax explained.

'Oh,' said Mandy.

'And they have a few tricks. Watch.' He stood up staring down at Henry one and Henry two. They quivered and squealed. 'Walky!' he said. They started to bark. 'Pee pee!' he said and they started to jump about a bit. 'Bone!' he said getting more enthusiastic. They barked and ran around in hectic nail-clattering circles. And then he said 'Walky, pee pee, bone!' several times and they went berserk. Very weird thought Mandy. Bob Lomax laughed as he made for the kitchen, his dogs jumping around him. Over his shoulder he said to her, 'My studio is downstairs, why don't you go and have a look round and I'll bring you some tea.'

He went into the kitchen surrounded by yapping and barking. There was a small darkened room in the basement. In the middle was a table on which a large folio lay open. There was a pile of drawings in the folio neatly mounted on grey card. At first Mandy didn't look at the drawings, she looked at the pictures pinned to the wall by the window. There were a couple of invitations to private views, a postcard of a mountain scene, a mug shot of Bob Lomax his face looking dead. Amongst all this was a pin-up the bosoms thrust out, the lips parted. Mandy turned away resisting an urge of which she was ashamed, an urge to look, a fascination she didn't understand. She turned towards the table and the drawings. Still put out by the soft porn nude, Mandy didn't focus properly on the drawings for a few seconds, when she did she was shocked. They were drawings of female forms, drawn with clinical precision and accuracy, each form made up of minutely perfected safety-pins. The female forms were all naked. Mandy looked through them. The first few were almost identical, and then there was one which really horrified her. A female form with her legs open and the vagina a nest of opened safety-pins. There was a hatred, an aggression, a fear in the drawings which Mandy didn't understand but which settled into her subconscious.

A little voice of instinct told her to creep up the stairs and out of the door, but Bob Lomax appeared. 'Tea?' he said and Mandy felt a sensation like an army of cold ants running up and down her spine. She looked down pretending to be interested in the drawings which had fallen back into place so a relatively mild safety-pin female form presented itself. Mandy wondered whether they got more violent and ugly as the pile deepened and was glad she didn't know. The poodles had followed Bob Lomax down the stairs. He was talking, leafing through the drawings saying dispassionately how this one had worked but that one still wasn't right. Mandy was struck by the oddness of this apparently ordinary looking person talking about these horrifying drawings as though discussing merchandise. The poodles milled around sniffing at her legs. Mandy reassured herself that this was someone her brother knew so he must be all right really. Probably it was just that Mandy didn't understand art or life. They did, they were adult men, artists and after all there was something flattering about being taken seriously. It was a novelty. He went on talking about his work, talking art terms about perspective and the relative merits of this kind of pencil or that kind of pen. He talked about the drawings as if they had nothing to do with real women, and Mandy noticed that these female forms had no faces, they were all blank. He suggested that they go upstairs to the living room and Mandy was relieved, supposing it would be warm and normal. The dogs clattered behind them and pushed past her on the stairs.

The living room was dark and gloomy because of the prolonged summer storm. The shutters weren't drawn back fully, they were the same grey as the sky. The room was grey, the chairs were grey. Mandy sat on the edge of a sofa, ill-ease creeping all over her. She wanted to leave but remembered that as she impulsively ran out of the restaurant with Bob Lomax, she hadn't picked up her bag so she had no money. It had been sunny when she left for work in the morning so she had no rain coat. She was wearing a cotton skirt and a tee shirt and had begun to shiver. Bob Lomax sat in the corner on a hard chair with wooden arms. He didn't speak. He fondled the poodles. Plunging about for something to say and feeling she was like someone caught in a mist, Mandy said, 'Why do you clip those poodles like that?'

'Why not?' he replied.

'Because they look so strange.'

'Do they? What do they look like?'

Mandy looked at them and the word doom came to mind.

'They look like . . .' she paused, 'they look like the poodles of doom.' She wondered how she'd come up with the phrase and surprised herself even more when she giggled.

He laughed. 'Poodles of doom, very good, ha ha.' Mandy stopped laughing. She contemplated the general air of doom, everything tainted with a kind of lifelessness. He was looking at her. She glanced at him. He still looked normal, which continued to surprise her. She rubbed her head. 'Are you all right?' he said.

'Well I've got a bit of a headache actually.'

She was about to say it was time she went home but he said quickly, 'I know a very good cure for headaches. I learned it in China.'

'Oh?'

'Yes, you lie down on this cushion,' he pointed to a large cushion, 'and I'll show you.' Mandy was reluctant to comply, she knew there was something wrong about lying on a cushion alone in a room with a man. But how could this normal person who had connections with her family intend anything but to help her get rid of her headache. Her reluctance was obvious so he said in a very sincere voice, 'I stay over here while you lie down and I just ask you questions, OK?' Mandy's head had really begun to thump. She lay down on the cushion. 'Now then, what shape is your headache?'

'It doesn't have a shape,' she said.

'Wrong, all headaches have shapes.'

'Rectangular,' she said in order to oblige.

'And what colour is it?'

'No colour.'

'It must have a colour.'

'OK, yellow, I don't know.' Her head was thudding with the effort of thinking. He came over and knelt beside her. She got up, pulling her skirt straight and pushing her hair out of her eyes. He stood up and they looked at each other, the cushion between them. A mixture of trust, innocence and lack of experience had stopped Mandy from running away. Something else too, a dangerous combination: curiosity and innocence. 'I want to go home,' she said. He said nothing. 'Can you take me home please?'

He looked at her. 'Home?' he said in a perfectly calm voice, so calm it was tinged with threat.

'Please take me home,' she repeated.

'Who said you were going home?' said Bob Lomax in his calm voice.

'Please take me home,' Mandy repeated, an unaccustomed blankness shutting out the rising fear. There was a short silence.

'Tea!' he said all jolly and normal again. 'Tea for a headache, let's have some more tea!'

'And then I'm going home,' said Mandy. He went to make more tea. Mandy looked round the room. There was almost nothing in it. But on the mantlepiece was a row of clarinets, or maybe they were oboes. They were standing up-ended. She was struck by their intricacy and thought they must be worth a lot of money. The poodles were watching her with bright little eyes. She returned their gaze with hostility.

Bob Lomax came in with the tea. 'Here we are, nice cup of tea.' He handed one to her. 'Feeling better are you?'

Mandy wondered if she had imagined the threat in his voice earlier; perhaps he hadn't said 'Who said you were going home?' because now he was sounding quite ordinary again. Mandy wanted to keep talking to fill the air with sound. She muttered something about getting headaches on stormy days and how the heaviness of it must have got to her. Talking relieved the strangeness. She asked him about the clarinets.

'They're oboes, it's a priceless collection, I used to play them.' Mandy had moved over to the mantlepiece; he had gone back to his chair. She floundered for something to say. Her ill-ease had returned and with it that sensation up and down her spine. She shivered. 'Oh dear, are you cold?' he asked, 'I'm sorry,' he was looking at her. Moments passed in silence as the light diminished and the rain continued to fall. He watched her, but she looked away.

The expression in his eyes unnerved her, something resigned but demanding, a sort of longing.

'Look, please, I'd like to go home,' she said trying again.

'No, please stay a little longer,' he said as calmly as before.

'No, I want to go, I want to go now,' Mandy said, her panic beginning to surface.

'But when there's someone here I don't feel scared,' said Bob Lomax. Mandy looked at him.

'What do you mean?'

He had begun to look frightened which alarmed Mandy even more. 'Sometimes my loneliness terrifies me.'

Mandy was frightened and bewildered but he was asking for sympathy and she felt she ought to be kind. The last thing she wanted was to stay there one second longer. She was about to make a move towards the door, but he anticipated this and before she could take a step, he stood in front of her. She stood very still staring back at him. There was desperation in his expression and determination. Hard eyes, grim mouth. He breathed rapidly. Mandy raised her arm and said, 'One move and I wipe your oboes off this mantlepiece', but before she could move he grabbed her. She fought, managing to make the oboes crash against each other and fall noisily to the floor. He was much stronger and pushed her roughly onto a sofa. He tore at her skirt and overcome by him she lay on her belly and then a terrifying pain went through her. As if from beyond herself, she heard a scream ripping through the greyness. Who was screaming, who was it? Again that scream and the pain. Mandy lost all sense of time but then realised the screams were her screams and began to fight; she lashed out, she kicked and struggled. He pinned her down and pinned her down until suddenly loosening his hold of her and groaning, he lay on top of her a dead weight. Mandy kicked and pushed her way from under him and ran noisily from the room grabbing the banisters and taking the stairs three at a time. The pavements were gleaming with rain and the sky was cold and grey. She ran along the street. He caught up with her, panting, pleading, apologizing.

A woman with shoulder-length auburn hair strolled along in the autumn sunshine on a Saturday morning, arm in arm with a tall man. They were very much at ease with each other, chatting, smiling, laughing. She had a strong face, not pretty but lively. They stopped and looked in shop windows and she pointed to this or that and he was amused by her extravagant fantasies. They had been strolling like this for half an hour or so when the man drifted on ahead of her, leaving her to contemplate a shop window full of second-hand books, a passion which he didn't share. He crossed the road, heading for a tobacconist, looking over his shoulder to see where she was. He gesticulated and she smiled and walked on slowly. Next to the bookshop was a small art gallery. She paused to look at the pictures in the window. She froze, an ugly memory slowly surfaced. 'Mandy' it was Eddy, who had rejoined her. She didn't reply. 'Mandy' he repeated. Still she said nothing. He put his arm around her gently, looking at her closely. She suddenly looked like a child, stricken and frightened. It was an expression that despite their fifteen years together, he didn't recognize. It wasn't like her to be quiet. Very occasionally, in certain moods, great sadness, white-hot anger, shame, she would withdraw into impenetrable silence. But this was different. What had happened in the five minutes since he'd gone to the tobacconist? Mandy stared at the pictures in the gallery. He tightened his arm around her, said her name again. Still no response. He tried to work out what she was staring at – perhaps it would explain this mood.

One picture was of a summer field, unremarkable. Another of fruit, a third an abstract image. There was another, a line drawing of a naked woman, the outline of her body all safety-pins. She didn't have a face. Eddy thought it was gruesome. 'Are you looking at the one with the safety-pins?' She didn't say anything but nodded slightly. 'Horrible isn't it?' She began to cry. 'Hey, Mandy what is it?' He held her close. She rarely cried, but now she clung to him, trying to suppress her tears. Eddy disentangled her hold and keeping an arm tightly around her, led her away, walking back along the street and into a park. He found a bench under the last of the summer trees and they sat down. He looked at her anxiously. Still she couldn't speak. Time passed, then eventually she whispered.

'Eddy' she began, 'You know that drawing?'

'The one with the safety-pins?'

'Yes. I knew that artist. It was a long time ago – it must be sixteen years.'

'Why did it make you cry? Is he dead?'

'I've no idea.' The thought of him being dead confused her – would she be glad?

'Did you like him?' Eddy asked.

'I never realized how much I despised him until now. Until I saw that picture.'

'Why?'

'Because I always thought it was my fault.'

'What was your fault?'

Mandy couldn't look at Eddy, she looked distractedly across the park to where some children played with a boat on a pond. They were trying to make it go by remote control but it just kept whirring and going in circles and then stopping, making phut phut noises. It held her attention completely for a moment. She thought how absurd to be interested in a toy boat at a time like this. She thought she'd be able to tell Eddy about Bob Lomax another time, to tell him fluently, to explain. 'I thought it was my fault, all these years, I thought it was my fault. I went there alone with him, I thought because I'd done that it was my fault.'

Again Mandy saw the oboes, tasted the tea, felt the gloom, heard the yapping of the clipped poodles. She saw a man with grey hair and an ordinary face. She saw the face harden, the mouth grim. She heard the scream, her scream and wondered if she was screaming there and then in the park, and then realized she wasn't. The children pulled their model boat out of the pond and clustered round it waving their arms. Eddy held her close.

Temple of Venus at Midnight

'Oh darling Maud, meet me at the Temple of Venus at midnight. Your adoring Rupert.' Maud read the note to herself under her breath. She looked out of the window as she folded it and put it in her shirt pocket. She had strange expressionless eyes, a heavy blue, long and lopsided set in a face that looked as if someone had put a hand either side of it and shifted its balance so that it had a warped look about it. She had white, smooth skin and heavy, silky blonde hair cut so that it curved above her wide, crooked jaw. She didn't talk much. In Rupert's Latin lessons he directed fleeting but pleading looks in her direction, which she either ignored or returned with her heavy inscrutable gaze. He had slipped the note into her essay as he returned it and paused a second longer beside her.

Jeannie glanced over at her just then and Maud wondered if she'd seen the note. Maud looked round at Ruby, who was drawing and had seen nothing. The lesson ended and Maud gathered up her books, still impervious to Rupert's little eyes trying to bore into her. He was a fat man with the remains of ginger hair plastered over his shiny bald head. His little lower lip jutted out below the upper one, and when he walked he tiptoed swiftly, bending forward slightly, like someone with a walk-on part in a play who always comes on at the wrong time.

Jeannie, Maud and Ruby were best friends. They strolled out of the classroom together and Rupert watched them go, hating Jean and Ruby, jealous of their easy intimacy with Maud.

Walton House was an exclusive progressive boarding school. The building looked out over vast sloping lawns, a lake and huge ancient cedar trees. Not far away, through a great field of corn, was a ruined castle. The school was designed for the daughters of rich artists, diplomats, princes from far-off lands, ambassadors, prime ministers from countries thousands of miles away. Art, music and literature, French, Russian and poetry were taught. Freedom of thought, imagination – these were the things the staff at the school were supposed to elicit in their pupils. In practice the schoool had become an orphanage for teachers who were unhappy, bizarre refugees from broken hearts and shattered dreams. The staff were, in short, odd.

The headmistress, Vera Calman, called Vera by the girls behind her back, had a misty thwarted past. She had knowing eyes and rarely displayed kindness. Her standards were double, treble, even, as inconsistent as the worst of opportunist politicians. She walked stiffly, her arms out at right angles as though permanently trying to get dry, and alongside her ran a little long-haired dachshund called Percy. Miss Calman's eccentricities determined the general air of repressed chaos. The school was run with a mixture of permission and oppression. While Miss Calman took one girl to the local family planning clinic to get contraception and then invited her to stay with her boyfriend in her flat for weekends, others were suddenly and severely punished for minor childish misdemeanours.

Maud, Ruby and Jeannie had bad reputations. Maud

never got caught. She was canny. Ruby frequently did and was permanently on the verge of being expelled, but Jeannie wasn't punished even if she was caught. The three girls sat in easy chairs in their commonroom as the evening drew to a close. Ruby was writing an essay for the only teacher she liked, Mrs. T., a middle-aged woman with nicotine-stained fingers who wore a sloppy grey suit with a certain elegance. Sparing with either praise or blame, speaking softly and hypnotically, Mrs T commanded respect.

Ruby was the most openly wild of the three. She was loud-mouthed, scruffy and plump, unable to resist a dare. Miss Calman secretly resolved to find enough evidence against her to send her home. Jeannie, who led the most protected life of the three, was very pretty, with a kind of young girl's magical beauty which reduced boys to a state of helpless adoration. She read avidly.

Maud watched her friends and surreptitiously pulled the note from her pocket. She spread it out carefully inside the atlas she was scanning (Maud loved maps) and weighed up the odds. She looked out of the large windows at the hills and summer meadows slipping into night. As the sun went down she tried to imagine what it would be like to feel his little lips pressed against hers and wondered whether he'd be like the men in the comic strip romances they read. Would he 'take her in his arms, press his lips to hers and say, Maud we were meant for each other'? She'd been reading some pulp where the hero was either called Jake or Brett and was 'ruggedly handsome', or he was a helpless, blushing gentleman called Nigel or Alexander, a decent sort, cut out for desk work and the occasional game of golf, who said 'Julia, be mine, I will show you the world.' The women in all the stories, even if they were a little bit sassy, always ended up compliant and submissive, the joyful, lucky recipients of hard-won male adoration and devotion.

Maud's reverie was suddenly interrupted by Rupert tiptoeing into the doorway and stammering that it was nearly 9 o'clock and they should be going to b-b-b-b-bed soon. Jeannie and Ruby started to giggle and Ruby said, 'B-b-b-but S-s-s-sir . . .' Rupert shot her a look of pure hatred. Maud regarded her suitor without expression. He shambled out of the room. Soon all the other girls had dutifully gone to their dormitories, but Maud, Ruby and Jeannie were still in their chairs.

'Shall we . . . you know?' said Ruby.

'What, crawling around the Rotunda without our clothes on?' said Jeannie, giggling as she remembered the expression on the face of the teacher on night patrol, when he saw Ruby's ample bottom wobbling just out of sight as she accomplished her dare.

'No,' said Ruby, 'boring, we did it before. How about a chair mountain?'

The other two looked at her in incomprehension. Ruby started pulling all the wooden upright chairs into the middle of the room and Jeannie joined in. Giggling, they built an enormous pile and then Maud climbed to the top.

'Let's put the bin under the pile and set fire to it!' said Ruby, who was given to occasional urges for mild pyromania. They put the bin underneath the pile and it had just begun to give off a thin line of smoke when Rupert appeared at the door. He blinked in amazement and then, still stammering, shouted at Ruby, 'This is your doing, you know no bounds, evil girl!' He started to run around the pile of chairs on his little tippy toes, bellowing at Maud to come down, using phrases like, 'I exhort you to descend.' Ruby and Jeannie laughed as he spluttered and careered about and put out the smouldering fire. Maud picked her way down the pile and the three girls ran from the room.

They were running along a corridor on the way to the

room they shared when they heard a reedy whimpering sound. It was Amanda, a sweet shy girl, a neurotic fifth year who looked anorexic. Miss Brockway, one of the matrons was shouting at her, 'Pull yourself together girl!' Amanda had bald patches in her hair, where through nerves, it had begun to fall out. She was cowering against the wall. Brock shook her, not too hard, just enough to shatter the little peace of mind Amanda had left. She started to weep uncontrollably and her best friend, who had been watching, led her away leaving Brock looking for other quarry.

Maud, Jeannie and Ruby rushed past her, making her flatten herself against the wall. Before she could stop them they were out of their dresses and into their nighties, combing their hair, wearing angelic expressions and smiling sweetly when she appeared at their door. She had been delayed by a quick stop-and-search interrogation on a passing girl. She glared at them, her tiny eyes glinting, and then swept out. There was something about Maud, and even more so Maud and her two friends, that filled Brock with a terrible rage. She didn't know how to handle them because they weren't frightened of her.

There were five minutes till lights out and the three girls went to say goodnight to their friends in the next dormitory. Brock appeared. 'Bed check,' she said in her sergeant major voice. 'Pull back the covers all of you instantly and let me see what you have hidden down these beds.' The girls reluctantly obeyed. She walked over to Celia's bed. Celia never caused trouble, but she wouldn't draw back the covers. 'Something to hide Celia?' barked Brock. Celia looked at her with a mixture of fear and hatred.

Ruby murmured repeatedly, 'Don't do it Celia.' The others in the dormitory looked on horrified but too scared to intervene. Brock swooped, ripping back the covers. Celia tried to cover her nakedness. It was a rule that nobody slept naked (except the girl allowed to make love in the headmistress' flat presumably). The reason went, 'If there was a fire what would local people think if Walton House girls were escaping with no clothes on!' Suddenly Brock raised an arm and brought it down savagely slapping Celia's thigh. The outline of a hand appeared as the thigh went red. The other girls froze and looked sidelong at Maud and Ruby, knowing they were the only ones with nerve for vengeance. They knew it would probably be Ruby who always acted on impulse.

'You bitch!' said Ruby, 'you sadist, you pervert!!!' The other girls' eyes glittered with delight.

'You will come here and apologize this instant!' Brock hissed. Ruby didn't move. 'How dare you,' Brock's hard and ample bosom was heaving under the starched white overall. 'You will come over here and apoligize or you will regret it. You are only at this school under sufferance and should have been expelled long ago.' Ruby raised herself very slowly from the radiator where she'd been sitting and strolled as insolently as she could across the room, swaggering a bit, pausing to wink at Celia as she passed her bed. Celia was still lying naked with the livid mark on her leg. She stood in front of Brock for a second, and then continued to stroll to the door. 'And where do you think you're going, my girl?' Ruby hated the way they called you 'My girl.'

'I'm not your girl, I'm . . .'

'What did you say?' snapped Brock threateningly.

'I said I'm not your girl and as to where I'm going, the loo.'

'Oh no you're not!' said Brock.

'Oh yes I am,' replied Ruby. Brock lunged forward and grabbed Ruby's arm. For the second time she had broken one of Miss Calman's rules: no rough stuff with her gells.

This, after all, was a modern, forward-thinking school, full of the daughters of the enlightened.

'You are going nowhere, my girl,' Brock's self-control was wound so tight it seemed it would snap.

Ruby lost her temper and screamed, 'Let go of me.' As Brock tried to hold Ruby back, and Ruby tried to get away, they somehow ended up in an accidental embrace. They waltzed down the corridor, a bizarre nightmare couple from some weird dancing competition. As they danced they exchanged furious comments through gritted teeth.

'You will not go to the toilet,' Brock said, her jaws tight.

'Oh yes I will,' replied Ruby.

There were clusters of excited girls in the doorways of the dormitories along the corridor. A tall girl began to sing 'Waltzing Matilda' and a few others joined in. Brock gripped harder onto her prey. Ruby yelled at her, 'If you don't let me go I will pee here and now!!!' With that she wrenched herself free and made a dive for the toilets, getting into one of the cubicles and slamming the door locked. Brock stormed about the big bathroom outside the loos. The chorus of singing and giggling faded as the girls went to their beds. Brock turned her back furiously and made for the matrons' sitting-room. She was met by the other matrons, the sad Miss Pickles, and the third matron, Mademoiselle Dubois, who was a favourite with the girls.

Maud stood just inside the door of Celia's dormitory watching Brock explaining furiously to Pickles and Mademoiselle what had gone on. Ruby, feeling lonely and abandoned in the loo, began to cry. She didn't want to come out in case Brock was still there. She knew she was beaten if Brock got her again. The three matrons went into their sitting-room, leaving the door open. The light spread into the corridor like a warning.

Maud got into Celia's bed and Jeannie into the next girl's

and they whispered while Maud planned the revenge. In the loo Ruby told herself what she always told herself when she was in trouble. She'd learned it when first sent to boarding school aged nine and was left lying in dark corridors late at night as punishment for talking after lights out. It went – this can't go on forever, nothing does. As a little girl she'd lain in the corridors telling herself this, the tears rolling down her face as she realized it meant one day her parents and everyone else, including most shockingly herself, would all be dead.

Maud knew Ruby well, and realized she had to be released quickly. Furthermore, if Maud was going to organize the release, not get caught, begin her revenge on Brock and meet Rupert in the Temple of Venus, she had better get on with it. Maud took up a position by the door waiting for the matrons to disperse. She could hear their voices. Pickles wearily said she'd go and get Ruby out of the loo. 'That girl . . .' Maud strained to hear but only caught the odd phrase, '. . . wild . . . broken home . . . haywire . . . sister's not like that . . .' and Brock's crisp, tight, nasty voice, '. . . no excuse . . . no manners . . . girl's bad.' then Mademoiselle's soft voice, harder to hear than the others, and she spoke for longer, 'not her fault . . . poor kid . . . stepfather drinks . . . kid's all over the place . . .' Then Brock snapped, her voice clear, 'For goodness' sake, you're so soft on these girls.'

Pickles made her way wearily along the corridor to the bathroom, where Maud could hear her saying, 'Ruby, come on now, come out, you've been a very naughty girl.' She couldn't coax Ruby out and soon gave up, appearing again in the dark corridor, muttering and sighing as she went. She had no taste for battle. She made her way heavily to the flat where she'd lived alone for twenty years. Soon after Mademoiselle emerged, said goodnight to

Brock and made her way down the stairs. Maud smiled. A few moments later Brock marched to her room at the far corner of the square corridor network.

'Jeannie,' Maud whispered, 'Celia, give it five minutes. She'll be in her dressing-gown by then.' Their ribs ached with suppressed laughter. The riot was used when something happened that some of the bolder girls didn't like, but it was used sparingly. Brock had been getting away with it for too long, her rule of fear had to be challenged. Safety in numbers meant Ruby would be able to get out with dignity. Maud, Jeannie and Celia each took a corridor, running swiftly from dormitory to dormitory, opening the door, flashing the lights and saying 'Riot!' The response was immediate. Within seconds a hundred teenaged girls were thundering along the corridors, whooping and yelling, faster and faster they ran, the excitement growing. Little shy girls, big bad ones, naughty ones, swots and studious ones, all joined the riot, inspired by revenge on Brock. She appeared, helpless and nasty, her turquoise brushed-nylon dressing-gown pulled tight over her ungiving body, with two tight little rollers newly dug into her scalp. Her arms flailed as she attempted to catch one girl and then another. But the girls were abandoned and absorbed, running amok in a wild delight.

Suddenly, like a film going into reverse, they all vanished into their dormitories, shut the doors, and pulled the covers up to their chins. Ruby, Jeannie and Maud were in their beds, gently snoring and snuffling in mock sleep when Pickles appeared for the showdown, shining her torch like a searchlight on their faces one by one. She scolded them in a half-hearted, defeated sort of way while Brock stood behind her like death. The matrons were forced into retreat by the mocking slumber of the girls.

Ruby, Maud and Jeannie bid each other goodnight. Jeannie and Ruby fell asleep very soon but Maud lay awake, staring into the darkness. After a while she got up and crept out of the room.

The school was silent apart from the sort of hum that comes from the breathing of a hundred sleeping girls. In her bare feet, Maud walked quietly along the corridors and down the double staircase beneath the great glass-domed roof. She slipped out through a side door and, under an almost full moon, made for the blackness of the spreading cedars. Maud had a nerveless quality; with acute animal instinct she glanced around her. Creeping through a stone archway into the secret garden edged by poplars and cypress trees, she strained her eyes as she paused behind a large camelia, its white flowers glowing faintly in the moonlight. She couldn't see Rupert.

'Maud!' he said, startling her as he tiptoed up from behind. He grasped her.

'Sir!' she exclaimed and he relinquished his hold.

'Rupert, call me Rupert, please,' he pleaded. He was breathing in little spasms, and Maud began to wonder why she was there. It didn't bode well for the first kiss, she thought. Despite her caution and wariness Maud was intrigued, with a clinical kind of curiosity, detached but intense. She was after all, only sixteen. It was the mixture of knowingness and innocence that so fascinated the teacher. A sphinx in a nightdress.

'Let us go to the Temple of Venus,' he said, picking up a picnic hamper. Maud knew he was making a fool of himself but now that she was there felt the necessity of seeing this through. He led the way through the dew-heavy garden, padding along on the tips of his toes. He ushered her to a stone bench in the gazebo and then began to orate poetry in Greek and Latin. He panted as he recited, then, castigating himself for his weakness and adoration, dropped to his knees and talked a lot of nonsense about her feet, the only part of her anatomy, apart from her hands and face, which wasn't under her nightdress and dressing-gown. Maud just sat there, her steady, impenetrable gaze fixed on his shiny face and anxious little eyes.

He opened the hamper and lifted out one delicacy after another: peaches, strawberries, champagne. With each offering he looked at her expectantly, hoping that she would give in to this seduction. From crystal glasses, which he explained had belonged to his dear dead mother, they drank champagne. Maud liked it, dipping the strawberries into her glass. Rupert sat beside her and when he quiveringly put his arm around her waist, she neither resisted nor responded but looked straight ahead, her heavy blue eyes without expression. She was thinking about Amanda and Celia, and about Ruby's bizarre dance with Brock. Her mind was working on how best to take revenge while her strange curiosity went its own way with the champagne and strawberries.

Ruby woke as the tongue of the bell in their room thudded stupidly against the sanitary towel she'd wrapped around it. She stretched and yawned and, blinking awake, saw Jeannie sitting on the edge of her bed rubbing her eyes. 'Where's Maud?' said Ruby. Maud always slept through the bell and usually missed breakfast. Jeannie looked round and saw Maud's clothes still lying on a chair. Wherever she was, she was still in her night things. 'Perhaps she's left us a note?' said Ruby, stumbling over to Maud's locker. Ruby was clumsy and hit her toes hard against the chair which fell over, scattering Maud's clothes. The note from Rupert, neatly folded in the shirt pocket, slipped out. Ruby, who could never resist reading letters and notes left lying around, unfolded it. 'What?! Jeannie look at this! "Meet me at the Temple of Venus . . ." what on earth?' She began to giggle. 'It's from Rupert. "Your adoring Rupert" . . . Jesus!'

'You don't suppose they've done it, do you?' said Jeannie.

'What . . . it . . .?'

'With Rupert!'

Jeannie and Ruby went looking for Maud. They worked out that the Temple of Venus must be the gazebo in the teachers' garden. Rupert had been careful; there was no trace of the picnic. They searched all the likely places: the chapel in the school catacombs where once they'd found Maud sleeping off a bottle of whisky; the pottery room where Maud liked to make clay models; all her haunts, but they couldn't find her. 'Do you suppose she's gone off, run away with him?' said Ruby. She thought Rupert was pathetic – not her idea of a 'real' man at all, nonetheless she felt jealous of Maud for having this older man's attention directed at her. Jeannie thought if you forgot about Rupert's little eyes and ridiculous tippy-toed walk, it was rather dignified to lose your virginity in a moonlit ritual with an older man. None of them had much sexual experience beyond clammy hand-holding and squashy kisses with boys in ditches and behind hedges, a practice commonly referred to as 'hedging and ditching'.

Walking back along a path under the dining-hall windows, Jeannie glanced in and saw the teachers and matrons, like the disciples at The Last Supper, sitting on a raised dais at a long table. Somebody was wiping the tables at the far end of the hall. Jeannie grabbed Ruby's arm. 'Oh no, Ruby, look!' Maud was swaying as she wiped the tables. She was wearing her nightdress tied round the middle to make it look like a summer dress. Her feet were bare. She was moving like someone in a ship on swelling waters. Brock was eating, head down, as she systematically pushed her daily ration of porridge into her little bat's mouth. Mademoiselle wistfully nibbled a piece of toast, gazing out over the lake, while Pickles worked her way through bacon and egg. Neither the matrons nor the few teachers that lived in had noticed Maud's peculiar behaviour. But it was only a matter of time. Ruby and Jeannie skirted the edge of the building and walked as quietly as they could into the dining hall. They went to the top and wiped the tables very fast. It wasn't unusual for friends to help the girls whose duty it was that week. Used to seeing these three together, the staff thought nothing of it. It had to be done before Brock finished her porridge. She wouldn't look up till then. They'd watched her eating before and knew she did it with complete devotion and concentration. Ruby and Jeannie closed in on Maud and, propping her up between them, took her quickly to the dormitory. Maud was laughing.

'Well, did you, you know with Rupert?' Ruby asked.

'How did you know I was with Rupert?' asked Maud.

'Sorry but we found this note he wrote you about the Temple of Venus.'

'Oh,' was all Maud would say as she kept on laughing.

'Well?' said Jeannie, 'Did you?'

'Did I what?' Maud wasn't going to tell them. 'I drank champagne and ate strawberries and peaches. And we had truffles. He proposed to me.' Maud laughed again, she had a throaty gravelly laugh, more of a chuckle really.

Jeannie started laughing but Ruby wondered exactly what it was Maud was hiding. There was something more, she had a feeling. 'What else did you do last night? Apart from the strawberries and so on? Did you stay out there all night? Or did he carry you off in his VW Beatle?' Maud smiled her blank, heavy smile. She nodded. Jeannie and

Ruby knew that they'd get no more out of her and the bell went for Assembly.

'Oh no, there's bound to be a huge lecture about the riot from Vera, all about the fees and our poor parents and the good name of the school and the bad influence on the younger gells.'

'Brock's playing the hymn,' said Maud, 'it's her week.'

'So what?' said Jeannie.

'Oh, nothing,' Maud replied carefully, brushing her thick fine blonde hair and looking at herself in the mirror.

'They can't punish anyone for the riot without punishing all hundred of us, that's the magic of it,' said Ruby triumphantly.

The assembly room was enormous, a ballroom in the days when some aristocratic dynasty lived there. The room had a very high ceiling and along one wall were windows from floor to ceiling. The walls were painted pale blue and covered in large portraits of lords and ladies with shiny porcelain skin and curiously lashless eyes. There were namby-pamby lords carrying braces of dead birds, and ladies dressed in ball gowns, their tiny toes poking out from the hems where little dogs sat daintily by the slippered feet of their mistresses. Vera came into the hall followed by the ubiquitous dachshund. The atmosphere was tense. Vera stared grimly through the rows of girls, her stern eyes resting on Ruby, Maud and Jeannie. 'Let us sing hymn number 129, "Jerusalem".'

Brock was sitting poised at the piano waiting for the signal to begin. Vera was the only person Brock tried to impress, and when she played the hymn she made a big show of her expertize with complicated chords and fancy trills. Vera raised her eyebrows slightly and looked at Brock who began the introduction, crashing straight in with the great groaning chords. There was a sort of dull thud on certain notes, a sound midway between a fart and a subdued squelch. Vera raised a hand and Brock stopped fighting with the keys. Vera walked across the front of the room followed by the dachshund, its little nails scratching as it scurried. Brock got up and helped her lift the lid off the grand piano, assisted by an embarrassed first-year who had been beckoned from the front row. All three peered into the strings. For a moment they froze. Then the first-year clamped her hand over her mouth. Vera solemnly told her to go back to her seat. She called a senior member of staff over to the piano and, like scientists, they peered at it. Overcome by curiosity, one by one other members of staff went over to the piano. Last was Rupert.

Word filtered back through the hall. There was a turd in the strings. Jeannie and Ruby joined in the general bedlam of laughter. Maud sat still, her expression as inscrutable as ever, smiling as all around her girls were nudging, gasping and clapping their hands over their mouths.

Vera emerged, waving her staff back to their seats and handed Brock a note she had found in the piano. The matron's face turned a deep red as she strode furiously from the hall watched by her embarrassed colleagues. Rupert leaned against the wall under a painting of a young dandy leading his horse through a wood, and looked at Maud who seemed to be looking straight through him.

Identity Parade

Michael wasn't part of the gang because he chose not to be but everyone liked him, even the tearaways who he never joined. He was a loner, a tall skinny eighteen-year-old with still, staring eyes. He was the youngest of four. Michael's parents had worked long shifts by day and night throughout their chidren's lives, and they had learned early to fend for themselves. He had three older sisters who were forever kissing, cursing or ignoring him unless they needed him to fetch and carry for them. He'd hear one of their voices raised in command 'Michael! Come here!' and he'd slip quietly out of the door and along the balcony of the old block where they lived. He'd sidle down the stairs as one or other sister appeared at the door yelling after him. Sharon stood at the door that day, her hair in rollers, dressed in a red slip and black high heels, shouting out her command. 'Go and get my dress from the dry cleaners! NOW!' and Michael was out of sight, down the stairs, round the corner and into the city heat of the scorched scrubby area the council called Wellington Park Estate.

'Hey Michael, where're you going?' It was Neil, tilting his hat to the back of his head.

'Nowhere,' said Michael, and they stolled along out of the estate and down to the canal path talking idly, easy in each other's company.

Down on the path under a bridge they met a group of

their friends, Winston, Frank and Steve. Neil slapped hands with Frank. 'What's happening?' he asked, looking round. Steve turned his sleepy eyes on his friend and smiled. 'Nothing, as usual.'

'Yeah, well, school's finished, got to find work,' said Winston. They all laughed.

Michael didn't. He was worried. His father had berated him the night before. 'My old man is on at me about a government course but I don't want to go on one of them,' said Michael.

'Yeah, YTS,' Winston grimaced.

'Better do what daddy says,' said Steve laughing, 'or you'll end up like me.' Steve was just home after three months in a detention centre.

'Yeah Steve, what *did* you do? I heard three different stories,' asked Michael.

'Gold bullion of course.' Steve looked up with a very serious expression on his face. 'Swiss bank account, you know, the usual stuff.' He grinned his amazing wide-tooth grin. 'Nah, nicked a car, you know how it goes, late one night, walking Angela home, wanted to impress her, tried a nice little white Escort, told her I'd been lent it for the evening by my uncle, got into a bit of a situation with a tree, a lamp post and another car.'

They laughed. Michael smiled, he'd never really felt like breaking the law.

'Sylv, could you come here?' Sid called up the stairs to his daughter. Sylvia was reading and tried to pretend she hadn't heard him calling. 'Sylv!' he said more loudly and insistently.

Sylvia heaved herself off her bed and poked her head crossly round the door at the top of the stairs. 'What?' she said.

'Would you go out and get me the evening paper and a packet of fags?' 'Would you' and 'could you' didn't invite the answer 'no'. Sid had always expected Sylvia to do certain things for him but never forced or threatened her. She had gone along with it for years but lately it had begun to get on her nerves. Why was Sid so lazy! She pushed her feet into her shoes and showed her irritation by stamping down the stairs more noisily than necessary.

'What are you doing up there anyway?' Sid asked.

'Reading,' she said.

'Can't see the point of reading myself and you, you're always stuck in some book. Far as I can see reading never paid no bills, I dunno.' Sid couldn't understand his daughter. Where did she get it from? He never read anything except the paper and he only read it for the football and racing results. When she'd got the paper he would consider the dogs and horses and having chosen he'd send her to the bookies with a fiver. 'Sylv, would you get a pint of milk while you're out, I'm dying for a cup of tea.' More of the 'would you', 'could you', Sylvia grumbled to herself. She missed her mother at times like this although it was ten years since she'd died.

'June's coming round tonight,' Sid said. June had been his regular girlfriend for a year. She was the main problem at home as far as Sylvia was concerned. Sylvia dreaded the thought of them marrying and June moving in. June's hair was dyed somewhere between pink and blonde. Her nails were long and painted a pearly silver, she wore plunging necklines and high heels and made an effort to speak like the TV announcers. Sylvia didn't trust her; June tried very hard with Sylvia, too hard.

Sylvia walked slowly along the hot dusty street. She was in no big hurry. It was a city summer night and people were out on doorsteps, leaning against walls and sitting on benches under trees. She decided to take a long way round, her father could wait. He was nice enough, a regular sort of man and an adequate father, but he made no attempt to understand her. Still, Sylvia thought of some of the stories girls at school told about their fathers and considered herself lucky. What about poor old Sharon who got strapped when her father felt like it? And Sukvinder who was always crying because her father had her cousin spy on her to make sure she didn't talk to boys? And Jane's father who walked off with another woman when her mother was eight months pregnant? Sylvia was quite fond of Sid really.

She had discovered the refuge of books soon after her mother's death and was well known by the local librarians who kept new novels under the desk for her so she could have them first. It was school holidays and she was starting work but she would go back to the sixth form for 'A' levels. Sid didn't understand, 'Why do you want to sit in a classroom? I couldn't wait to leave school.' Sylvia followed her urge to study, she dreamed of escape, of some college far away from the monotony of home and life with Sid, and especially now with June hovering, Sylvia felt the need to escape.

'Thieves, thieves!! Murderers! Muggers!' A terrified elderly voice ripped through Sylvia's reverie. Just above her was an old woman leaning out of a window screaming. Without a second thought, Sylvia ran up the steps and in through the door which was open because it had been forced. Sylvia fought the revulsion she felt as she ran up the stairs, there was a strong sour smell. She went into the dishevelled flat. The old woman was hysterical, leaning out of the window, crying and thumping her fists on the sill.

There was debris everywhere, carrier bags and rubbish,

and two terrified cats cowered in a corner. There was a stench of rotting food and blocked drains. The old woman turned and saw Sylvia, 'Took the rings off my fingers, muggers, murderers'! she shouted angrily. Sylvia went over to her and put an arm around the old woman's thin heaving shoulders.

She glanced out of the back window and saw two men running away along the tow path behind the house. One had bright blond hair that bobbed as he ran and the other who was wearing a beige hat briefly looked back. The blond one was carrying something big and the other was trying to contain the contents of his bulging pockets without dropping a carrier bag. In this short time half the neighbourhood seemed to have crowded into the tiny flat. Sylvia sat on a settee thick with grime and cats' hair, the old woman now clinging to her. Several people were leaning over her trying to calm her down. Two women stood at the door, their arms folded. 'I thought I heard something, so I came to see what was going on, poor Mrs Turbutt,' she nodded knowingly. 'Well, you never know these days,' and then she whispered something. Sylvia heard a couple of phrases, 'Screw loose . . . not all there . . . never washes . . . won't have a home help . . .'

Four large policemen arrived and everybody stopped talking. Their walkie-talkies buzzed and beeped as they spoke into them. The old woman was crying noisily and still holding tightly onto Sylvia. One of the policemen leaned over the old woman. 'Now then, Mrs Turbutt, tell us what happened – and we'd like descriptions of the men please.'

Mrs Turbutt looked at him wildly. 'I don't know, I don't know, they ran past me, I came in, they ran past me, I'd been out, then one of them, he grabs my hand and pulls my rings off, I didn't look at them, I didn't see them, I wouldn't know.' She rubbed her old bony finger where the rings had been for years, leaving an indentation.

One of the women, who had been standing importantly at the door with her arms folded, came forward. She took the officer aside. 'My name is Maureen Briggs, officer, and Mrs Turbutt is my neighbour.' She lowered her voice slightly. 'She's, well you know, not herself, she wouldn't know what they looked like, even if she did she couldn't be relied on to tell you properly.' Maureen was whispering loudly, enjoying the drama and her role in it. 'She goes out wandering and picks things up out of bins and gutters, she's, well, you know,' Maureen whispered meaningfully, inclining her head on one side and repressing a sympathetic sigh. Turning to her friend, Mary, she said, 'This lady and I think they were black; we think we heard her say black mugger.' The two women nodded.

'These ladies say they think the burglars were black,' he said resuming his position bending over Mrs Turbutt.

'Were they?' she asked querulously. 'Oh I don't know, I don't know.' she said rocking from side to side.

The policeman looked at old Mrs Turbutt and then at Sylvia who hadn't said anything. 'Did you see anything?' he asked Sylvia.

She thought of the men she had seen running away. 'Yes, I saw two men running along the tow path out the back.' Everyone listened except Mrs Turbutt who wailed quietly and rocked gently from side to side. Sylvia looked out of the window again, the men had gone and she noticed a group of boys talking and laughing and fooling around down by the railings.

'Could you say what they looked like? Were they black?'

'One had blond hair. They were running, the other one looked over his shoulder, he was wearing a hat.'

'Was he black?'

Sylvia ran through what she had seen. She thought he had dark skin but wasn't sure. Instinctively she didn't like being asked these questions and wished she'd seen nothing. She looked up at the policeman. 'He might have been, I'm sorry, I'm just not certain. I think he might have had dark skin, it all happened so quickly.'

'Were they carrying anything?'

'The blond one was carrying something and the other one had a carrier bag. I think he was trying not to drop something in his pockets. But I'm not sure.'

The policeman made some notes while Mrs Turbutt went on whimpering. 'Thank you, we will want a statement from you later.'

Sylvia nodded.

'Group of black youths by the canal,' said an officer who had come forward, having made an inspection of the flat and looked out of the back window from where he saw the boys down by the canal.

Michael laughed when Steve described the noise the stolen car made as it hit the tree, then the lamp post and then a large new Volvo. 'But Angela won't speak to me anymore,' he said wistfully, 'and I really reckoned her, you know. Did you see the gold bracelet I gave her on Valentine's Day?'

Neil gave Gus a friendly shove, 'Come on now don't start crying or I'll push you in the canal.'

'I'd prefer it if you could put in a word for me to Angela, after all she is your cousin.'

'Angela has a fit if I even mention your name,' Neil explained. Steve looked at his shoes. He wore velvet slippers with gold initials embossed on them. Neil looked at them. 'Where'd you get those shoes anyway?' Steve carefully wiped one with a white handkerchief and gave his friend one of his special grins.

Beside the canal was a steep slope thick with summer grass and wild city flowers. A canoe went by paddled furiously by a red-faced sweating man. Dogs sniffed around and lifted their legs. Occasionally someone would come along the tow path on a bike and the friends would step back. It was summer, the evening was calm and warm. They were about to shift off and go back to Neil's flat with a few cans; they were in no hurry. They'd grown up together, gone to the same school, lived on the same estate, were easy together like brothers. It was nice to hang out watching the canal as the sun set, taking their time.

'Here you, sonny.' A policeman appeared at the top of the grass bank, then another and another. They came over the bank like a private army, threatening in their dark uniforms. The gang of friends fell silent; they were leaning against the railings in a line, looking either at their feet or abstractedly along the canal. Instinctively they didn't look at the police. The officer who was in charge and who had said, 'Here you, sonny,' repeated it as he approached Michael, who he seemed to have singled out. 'Yes, you, sonny,' he said again, like someone auditioning for a TV cop melodrama. Michael looked up then and steadily returned the man's glare, his expression betraying very little. He didn't like them, he knew how they treated young people like him but he'd never been picked on before. There were beads of sweat on the policeman's upper lip as he leaned over pushing his face close to Michael's. Michael involuntarily wrinkled his nose. 'Something offends you does it, Sambo?' said the police officer. 'I'm talking to you, boy,' repeated the officer. 'What's your name?'

'Michael Parker.'

The policeman scribbled in his notebook.

'Address?' Michael gave him the address. 'Date of birth?'

'What's this for?' Michael asked.

'You're under suspicion . . . you and your pals here, breaking and entering, half an hour ago. Where have you hidden the stuff then?'

'What stuff?' said Michael, cool and expressionless.

'Now I don't need to tell you that, do I?' Michael said nothing. His friends looked hard into the distance. 'Or do I . . . Sambo?' When he repeated the word 'Sambo', he hissed on the 's' and accentuated the first syllable, Ssssaaambo. Still Michael didn't rise to the bait. His mind went blank. All he felt was relief that they weren't picking on Steve. Steve would have given them faster lines back than they'd have known how to cope with, short of instant arrest. 'I take it I have to tell you then, do I?'

Michael returned the officer's look with calm and detached contempt. 'No, you don't need to tell me anything because I haven't done nothing,' said Michael.

'I haven't done nothing, is it?' His eyes narrowed to little fleshy slits, and as he spoke he sprayed a fine cloud of spittle into Michael's face, he was that close. Michael leaned back on the railings, his temper still held in check.

'What about the others, Sarge?' said a very keen, very young policeman.

'Search them,' said the arresting officer, keeping his eye on Michael.

'You, empty your pockets.'

Michael's pockets were full, he was carrying his keys, some money, a mouth organ of Neil's that he'd brought to return to him, and some old chocolate wrappers shoved into his pockets one day when there wasn't a bin around (Michael was no litter bug). He had a large screwed up handkerchief and a letter from an aunt in the West Indies.

He was embarrassed pulling this peculiar collection out and displaying them to the policeman's scrutiny. The other policemen were searching Neil, Steve, Winston and Frank. Nothing was found. Their names and addresses were taken. The arresting officer had some special interest in Michael which Michael couldn't understand.

All the boys were frisked and then the arresting officer said, 'Alright let them go – for the time being. But you Michael Parker, are coming with me.'

'Why?' said Michael, upset and frightened but determined not to show it.

'Because, Sonny, you are wearing a hat.' Michael had his fawn coloured tam on over his hair. 'And, so was one of the suspects.'

'See over there at the back of the estate? See that poor old lady?' There was an old woman peering from behind a curtain on the first floor of one of the houses that backed onto the tow path. She seemed to be cursing him. 'Yes, poor old lady,' the officer continued. 'Defenceless pensioner. Well, someone has been in there and stolen her bit of money and her pension-book and took her portable TV as well, and then pulled the rings off her fingers before making off with the lot, poor old dear,' his voice oozed with pantomime sympathy.

Michael glanced round at his friends and the other policemen. The officer-in-charge led Michael up the grassy bank. Frank called out, 'See you soon,' and the others called after their friend reassuringly. The police officers scrambled after them shoving their notebooks in their pockets.

Going down to the station in the squad car, Sylvia was scared. She tried hard to remember exactly what she had seen and replayed the glimpse of the two men running away. An ambulance had come for Mrs Turbutt and she had been led away as her hysteria subsided into a distressed, mumbled litany, 'I don't know, I don't know,' she kept saying as she stared around her. The squad car went fast, its flashing lights adding to Sylvia's alarm. She looked out of the window as the car sped past streets she knew well, past shops with which she was familiar, past the school she would be going back to in September. As the light faded and night fell, those familiar streets seemed strange and distorted. The officers in the car didn't speak to her. They had asked her politely to go down and make a statement and she had agreed automatically.

'Now then, we've got a young lady here who says she saw two men running away. Not,' he said looking Michael up and down 'that I'd call you much of a man. No hair on your chin yet, is there? Or does it come later with you people?' Michael stared at the wall behind the policeman's head. He didn't want to meet the provocation. He'd heard about this routine from other young men who'd been picked up. Don't give them a chance to get under your skin, he told himself. Don't let them wind you up. Don't let them see that you want to hit them. Don't let them see that you want to cry, don't let them . . . He repeated these phrases over and over to himself.

'Can I see a solicitor?' he said.

The policeman laughed. He went on laughing. 'Oh we want our solicitor, do we?' he said making mocking faces. 'It's the cells for you tonight, my lad, and tomorrow the identity parade, you'll enjoy that!' Michael fought back tears of rage and fear as they locked him in the cell.

After she had given her statement the police took Sylvia home. They chatted to her saying how difficult it was these days fighting petty theft and local crime. Sylvia didn't want to talk to them; she wanted to be home and forget what had happened. She was upset. Sid came to the door when the squad car drew up. The driver got out. 'Mr McClaren? Good evening, Sylvia has been very helpful. If you wouldn't mind, we'll just come in for a moment and explain.' Sid listened attentively as they explained what had happened and said that they'd like her to attend an identity parade in the morning.

June went straight into action. She preened and smiled and made the two officers cups of tea and produced biscuits served on plates with paper doilies under them. Sylvia thought the appearance of the doilies was bad news; June was staking out her patch. If she moved in, the toilet seat would have one of those stupid hats on and there'd be a poodle in an overcoat. Just then, she heard the officer saying, '. . . and so you see Mr McClaren, it seems Sylvia was the only one who saw them.' Sid nodded and looked at his daughter. 'Well, that'll be all. We'll come for Sylvia at 11 o'clock in the morning if that's all right with you.' Sylvia looked at her father.

June had got up and was fussing over the policemen as she saw them out, saying, 'Of course we're only too happy to help in any way we can.' Sylvia didn't like the use of the word 'we'; she wondered if it meant that her father had proposed to June.

Michael shivered despite the hot summer night. The cell could never be anything but cold. On the walls previous occupants had scratched their initials and the names of girls. 'Mick 4 Sue' and 'Steve luvs Lin'. Michael had never had a girl and wished he had so he could think of her and the comfort he'd get from her when he got out. They'd taken his belt and the laces from his trainers. They'd told him to empty his pockets and had taken his fingerprints. They made him sit in a chair and turn his head to left, right and centre while they took his picture. He stood silently while the arresting officer went through the formality of explaining to the custody officer why Michael was under arrest. 'Suspect held on suspicion of theft from an old lady, a Mrs Turbutt. Evidence is he's wearing a beige hat and so was suspect seen running away by witness, Sylvia McClaren.' Michael thought he saw a smile hover on the arresting officer's face. Throughout this humiliation he said nothing. He was determined to keep silent. The officer who had been taunting him from the start left him with one last sneer, 'You'd best be getting used to life behind bars, Sonny.' Michael stared at the grafitti, reading it over and over again.

He didn't know how long he'd been asleep when some-one shook him gently, and he woke thinking he was at home and his mother was trying to raise him. A man's voice said softly, 'Here you are Michael, nice cup of tea.' Rubbing his eyes, Michael sat up. Beside him was a man in ordinary clothes, smiling kindly. 'How are you? I hope you didn't get roughed up too much?' Michael hadn't been physically hurt, the assault was verbal and the damage psychological. He looked at the man suspiciously. 'So, Michael, got yourself into a spot of bother, haven't you?' Michael wondered if they got their chatty little phrases out of some special manual, 'spot of bother' was one such phrase. 'Best tell me all about it,' he went on. 'It won't be so bad if you admit it, plead guilty. We might even be able to get it heard in the Crown Court and not the magisrate's if you like. After all, you haven't got any previous, have you?' The only time Michael had ever heard that one, 'previous', was on 'Minder'. He almost smiled. 'Feeling better? Good,' purred the detective, taking advantage of the hint of a smile. Michael's face closed again, resisting the wiliness of the intruder. 'Just sign a statement saying who was with you and that you were there as accomplice and we'll let you out of here. OK? Cigarette?' he said, offering one to Michael. Michael didn't smoke. He said nothing. He felt disorientated, he wondered if his mind was playing tricks on him and wished again that he had the name of a girl to hang onto, like a prayer. 'Mick 4 Sue'. He looked at the wall. 'Steve luvs Lin.' He conjured up images of girls called Sue and Lin, he saw open, fresh smiling faces. He imagined them lying in a meadow with their shirts open, he imagined the comfort, the bliss . . .

'Well don't say I didn't warn you,' the detective sighed theatrically as he got up, feigning regret. 'I'm very sorry to see a nice young fellow like you get yourself into a lot more trouble than you need to. A few names, a couple of addresses, perhaps a drug dealer or two and we could even arrange to drop the charges. But . . . We'll have to do the identification parade you know, and it's your right to choose. Either you go on the parade or you can be confronted by the witness. Take your pick.'

Michael imagined the witness being brought to his cell and the thought alarmed him despite his great desire to see someone from the real world. But another stranger, one possibly hostile to him, what if she (he'd heard a girl's or woman's name mentioned) panicked and said it was him, what if she'd been talked into it. He thought of an identification parade, he'd seen them on TV dramas, a few guys standing in a line and someone slowly walking past them. Nobody could possible pick him out, and there was always the chance the guy he was supposed to resemble might be on the line.

'Well?' said the detective.

'The parade,' Michael said, his voice a little hoarse, it

was a long time since he'd spoken.

'Right, tomorrow morning. Think about it though, a couple of names, a little information and the charges will never even be written down. Think about it.' Michael's face was closed off to the man, he turned and looked at the wall.

The detective stood up. He tapped on the door as he gave one last sigh, looking at Michael. The door was opened and the detective slipped out, pausing in the doorway and stubbing his cigarette out under his heel. The door banged shut again leaving Michael staring at the wall.

'Send them back,' June said puffing herself out. Sylvia looked at her steadily, making no effort to hide her contempt. Troublemakers, delinquents, muggers, bringing the neighbourhood into disrepute,' June went on. She was clucking and tutting, oblivious of Sylvia or how she might be feeling after what had just happened. 'There was one next door to me got herself pregnant; they breed like rabbits, like the Irish. Got herself pregnant just so's the council would have to rehouse her, oh they never marry, do they? I said she should have an abortion. I went round there and told her, well, I thought she might not know about things like that and I'd be doing her a favour. I didn't like talking to one of them mind you, but she should have had an abortion. And she gets benefits, she got a free cooker. I've worked my fingers to the bone for everything I've ever had. Nobody gave *me* charity I can tell you! Mark my word, June Masters pays her own way!' Her head wobbled with righteous indignation.

'The trouble is they're naturally criminal, it's where they come from, how they're brought up, they don't know any better,' she went on. 'It's bred into them, noisy parties, drugs. I know, I've seen how things have changed here since they arrived. I've seen it with my own eyes, and it's worse than ever now because they won't work; they're lazy and so they take to a life of crime. Send them back, that's what I say.' She paused briefly, pursing her lips and flicking a piece of imaginary dirt from her pink nylon and angora sleeve. 'And bring back the death penalty,' she finished with vehemence. Sid turned on the TV as June's outburst ended. She was restraining herself; she didn't want to put Sid off. He was a good catch for her. Sylvia went to her room and lay on her bed for a long time just thinking about everything that had happened.

Michael's mother, father and three sisters went to the police station. 'Please may we see our son?' Mr Parker asked the duty officer politely.

'My son has never done anything wrong, he is innocent!' said Mrs Parker. She began to cry and Michael's eldest sister, Elizabeth, put her arm round her mother. The two younger sisters, Sharon and Miriam, stood close by. Miriam had hold of Sharon's hand, worried that she would explode if they were refused permission to see Michael.

'I'm sorry but instructions are no visits tonight,' said the officer.

'He's got a right to see his parents!' Sharon flared up.

'I've got my instructions and the superintendent has gone off duty, rules are rules, no visits tonight.'

Mr Parker asked again, 'Please could we see our son, I am asking you as one man to another, and perhaps you have a son of your own, to let my wife and I see our boy.'

'Rules are rules, no visits.'

Mrs Parker cried as the family walked home in the dark. Elizabeth, Miriam and Sharon were bursting with anger.

It was very dark in Sylvia's room as she lay on her bed with her hands behind her head. The impersonal coldness and shabbiness of the police station had unnerved her. She felt very lonely. Downstairs she heard the drone of the TV and the occasional muffled voice of her father replying to June's higher note. June's voice edged on shrillness, and Sylvia drifted into memories of her mother's soft voice and gentle hands. Nobody had hugged or kissed her for years and until that moment she hadn't fully realized how much she missed physical affection. She turned over and gazed at the picture on her bedside table. A kind pale face, a fading photograph, elusive.

She had seen identity parades in films. Someone walking slowly past a line of men all staring sternly ahead, never looking at the person scrutinizing them. She dreaded it. What if she got the wrong guy? She saw the two fugitives, the blond head of one and the awkward movements of the other as he struggled with the bag. She wished she had a boyfriend, someone to put his arm round her and reassure her, to murmur to her softly and stroke her hair. After her mother's death, Sylvia retreated into herself, became quiet and contemplative. She spent a lot of time alone, tuned into her imagination where she lived vivid fantasies, sometimes identifying with the leading character in the novel she was reading. Her apparent remoteness and her self-contained manner made others restrained with her; they didn't try to get close because she seemed not to invite them to. But she wanted close friends. She wanted to be noisy and foolish, to dance and laugh loudly and be part of someone's gang. She heard her father and June clattering dishes in the kitchen and tried to shut their voices out. June was washing up; she was intruding more and more. Sylvia got out the novel she was reading and disappeared into another world.

Michael stood in line with seven other young men who like him, were black. They avoided each others' eyes, but it was easy to guess that Michael had spent the night in the cells. He was led out to the yard last and there were no laces in his shoes. The yard was surrounded by grim walls snarled along the top with bits of broken glass and barbed wire. Michael had slept a strangely deep sleep and felt dazed. His mouth tasted thick and furry and his eyes were heavy.

An Inspector Michael hadn't seen before appeared with a young girl and led her into the yard. She must be the one they claimed had seen him at the old lady's house. Michael looked at her. He liked her face. It was ordinary at first glance but there was something about her which attracted him. What a depressing irony. It was rare for him to want to make contact with a girl and yet here he was, perhaps about to be singled out by her as a criminal. Michael wondered if his mind was going; maybe he wasn't drawn to her at all but the ordeal of the night was taking its toll and he was losing control of himself, imagining things.

The officer in charge stepped back and Sylvia was told to start walking along the line. She reluctantly inched forward and then turned away. She was escorted along the line by an inspector. As she turned away he quietly urged her back to face the line. The power she had turned Sylvia's stomach. She had to force herself to look at the first young man then the second and the third. She looked quickly, feeling relieved not to recognize them. Michael was sixth. Just as she was going to look up at him, the Inspector coughed and cleared his throat. Involuntarily, Sylvia turned her head and glanced at him, she thought she saw him nod very slightly, she wondered if she imagined it. Michael was very scared. He felt he could hardly breathe. Sylvia looked at him and moved straight on. Michael watched her shake her head when she'd finished, addressing the gesture to the

Inspector. He looked angry. For the first time it struck him
that the police really did think it was him who had broken
into the old woman's house. He wanted to cry, could feel
his throat tighten. He wanted to protest his innocence.
As Sylvia was led away he looked at her again and saw how
pale she was, how subdued. He felt sorry for her.

When Michael was released the entire Parker family was
outside the station waiting for him. Elizabeth, Sharon and
Miriam yelled when he appeared and his mother wept as
she put her arms around him. His father patted him on the
back as they walked away. Elizabeth had been burning
with anger since the arrest and, shaking her fist as she
made her way down the road, she looked over her shoulder
and said, 'We'll get even, we'll get compensation for this!'
Over lunch Michael recounted the details and Elizabeth's
anger grew. Sharon and Miriam joined her. They raged,
they wanted revenge. Their parents tried to pacify them;
the charges had been dropped, no trouble, no trouble, all
these years we've turned our faces away from the abuse,
please, please, no trouble.

June had moved in. As Sylvia had feared, in just two weeks
the house had begun to look like a mixture of reproduction
antique warehouse and third-rate swanky hairdressing
salon. The toilet got its hat. There were porcelain figurines
of damsels in frilly frocks which June endlessly dusted
and worried about. There was a fat pedigree cat, white,
enormous and fluffy, with a pink ribbon in its fur. The
settee was covered in primpy little cushions and the plain
net curtains replaced by dreadful stuff that looked like
knickers.

Sylvia's resentment grew day by day. Evidence of June
was everywhere; the bathroom was full of powders and
bottles and pungent sickly aromas. She felt she would

suffocate under the nets and frills and statuettes and the prim little cushions. June's insincerity sickened Sylvia, who now spent her days in parks and libraries or drifting around shops and markets. It was a relief to start her job at the checkout of a large local supermarket. The monotony and ceaseless clamour dulled the rising panic she felt and the casual friendliness of the other girls on the tills soothed her nerves.

Sylvia had sunk into a kind of torpor at home. She followed her whims and heard only what she wanted to, developing a way of shutting herself off from June's simpering and sentimentality. Very occasionally June's face cracked to reveal a jarring viciousness which she tried to hide from Sid. Sylvia saw through June's overtures to her. June was keeping up pretences just until Sylvia left home. She didn't like Sylvia. Sid seemed oblivious to all this. Sometimes Sylvia would look at him and find him faintly ridiculous. She'd see him as though he were a stranger. Who was this man she'd lived alongside for so many years? All too often she saw a man who'd given in and it worried her. June's intrusion into her life and the business about the break-in and the identity parade had reawoken the pain which had lain dormant. She could feel it just below the surface of her consciousness. The methodical work at the supermarket kept it submerged as she rang up the goods – 60p. £5. £5.25. £3.99 – mathematical lullabies day in, day out. She did overtime and in the evenings read books. She walked home slowly along the canal or through the side streets, extending the journey, lost in dreams.

Michael smiled. It seemed the first day he'd come out of the depression after the arrest. Elizabeth was yelling for him, 'Michael!! Come here!' He dropped the paper he'd been flicking through and instead of sidling out in search of

peace and quiet, he went willingly in search of his screaming sister. 'Michael, I need some hairspray, go and get
some for me, please, I'll pay you.'

He laughed. 'Leave it out, I'm not thirteen anymore,
just ask, I'll go for you, I need some things anyway.' She
cuffed him over the head affectionately and he ducked,
grabbing her and tipping her backwards onto the settee.

Michael was so used to getting things for his sisters,
female things, personal, intimate girls' things, that he
didn't feel at all funny when he got to the checkout.
Without looking up he put down the hairspray, some nail
varnish which Miriam had asked for, cotton wool and
eye make-up remover pads that Sharon wanted. He'd got
himself some batteries and four bars of chocolate. The girl
at the checkout glanced up at him and smiled as she rang up
the nail varnish. He smiled back and then suddenly his
heart did a panic beat. It was the girl from the parade.

He stood there paralyzed, ransacking his mind for something to say. He considered saying thank you and hello how
are you, or it's been a long time or I liked your face the
minute I saw you, but they all seemed absurd and silly. She
was waiting patiently for his money and the people in the
queue behind began to shift irritably at his hesitation.
The girl looked at him steadily, no flicker of recognition,
and repeated, for the third time, '£8.65 please.'

The man behind him said, 'Get a move on son,' and began to push him as he unloaded his trolley.

'It is you!' Michael said finally. 'It is, I know it is!' She
looked perplexed. 'It is you, isn't it. You're her, aren't
you?' Michael blundered on. Sylvia smiled. There was
something comical about this young man with his big eyes
and peaked cap, standing there all confused and jumpy.
'What time do you finish work tonight?' he said, as the man
behind began to grumble seriously. 'Eight thirty' said

Sylvia looking up at Michael with amused curiosity.

At eight twenty-five Michael was standing outside the supermarket bouncing from one foot to the other. He peered intermittently into the brightly lit shop. Girls were leaving in twos and threes, chattering and laughing. He pressed his nose to the glass. There she was! She appeared from the back of the shop pulling on her jacket. She turned her head, someone must have spoken to her, and she smiled. He was almost bouncing into the air with nerves by the time she got outside. She smiled and he fell into step beside her.

'I . . . I . . . I . . .' he began.

'Yes?' she replied.

'I . . . I . . . I . . . my name is Michael Parker.'

'I'm Sylvia McClaren.'

'OK,' he said, furious with himself for his confusion.

'I don't know you, do I?' said Sylvia.

'Well, not exactly, but I know you . . .' Sylvia was thinking hard. 'You were the girl at the identity parade.'

Michael was suddenly terrified that because he'd been on the parade she would think he was a criminal. It got to you like that. Sylvia smiled at him warmly then. 'I still don't recognize you. I hated that identity parade.'

'Hey, Sylvia, spend some time with me? Let's go and have a hamburger?'

Sylvia got home much later than usual. Her father's only rule was that she had to be in by midnight unless she'd warned him she'd be later. But it was months since she'd been in after nine thirty. June and Sid were watching TV. It was June who asked her where she'd been. Sylvia was glowing with a joy she'd forgotten existed. She wanted to protect it from June's poison. She lied, saying she'd been back to one of the other girls' houses for a cup of tea. Her father smiled and went on watching TV. June pursed her lips. 'Well, I don't know, a young girl out late and unaccounted for . . .'

Sylvia closed her bedroom door and sat on the edge of her bed feeling a huge and terrible happiness. She had never felt so much at ease with a boy as she had with Michael. He made her laugh, made her feel warm. She felt as though her whole being was expanding, as if she'd been held in very tightly for as long as she could remember without being aware of it. She felt a tremendous excitement as though her life was about to change.

Michael had wanted to be gallant. He went to get the hamburgers, and dropped them and had to start again. He managed not to spill the milkshakes or coffees but he suddenly felt foolish. He began to apologize, but wiping the last of the milkshake off her mouth and gurgling up the last frothy bubbles with her straw, Sylvia laughed. She was different when she laughed. It wasn't just that her face came alive, the whole world came alive. Michael felt that the little table under the neon strip lights was the whole world and he laughed too. She had told him about Mrs Turbutt and the police and June and her mother and father. She spoke animatedly, like someone who had been gagged for months, spilling the words into the air. He walked her home, dying to hold her hand or put an arm around her, but his experiences with girls were confined to fumbling and mumbling and hopeless, wretched, embarrassed collisions of noses. He couldn't decode girls' messages, but with Sylvia it was different. She felt like a friend and he had a sense that there'd be plenty of time for kissing.

When he got home everybody was out or in bed except

for Elizabeth who was in the kitchen reading a glossy magazine. He came in noisily, banging the door after him. He made for the kitchen and Elizabeth looked up, 'Don't vex me Michael, don't make so much noise!' she said frowning, she looked at her brother. 'That hat! How come you wear it all the time, who do you think you look like?' Michael thumped her playfully and she grabbed him by the wrists. She was surprisingly strong and forced him into a chair beside her. 'Where've you been? You're so frog-eyed and stupid looking. I haven't seen you like that since you won the break-dancing when you were thirteen.'

'You ever been in love, Elizabeth?'

'Of course I've been in love! But don't tell me my little brother has fallen in love!'

It wasn't that Sylvia felt she had anything to hide from her father, but since June had moved in she had felt even less able to tell him anything. Although they had never really had conversations, Sylvia and Sid had co-existed peacefully enough over the years. She had never thought about him very much, never seen him as a man, only as her father. He had always been rather silent. With June's arrival he was forced to respond occasionally, but only occasionally as June preferred the sound of her own voice to anybody else's. All she needed was a 'yes' or 'no' or 'is that so' to keep going for hours. Sylvia avoided June and Sid. Her father didn't ask where she was; he felt his daughter could look after herself; she always had.

One night as Sylvia came in from work she heard June's high-pitched tone, a tone overlaid with the kind of sweetness that holds candy floss together. Sid and June were having a meal. June was saying, 'And I told Mrs Parfitt that I didn't think it was right, a young man of his age carrying on like that, there's no excuse.' Sylvia walked into the kitchen. 'Sylvia dear, hello,' said June without a trace of genuine warmth. Sylvia greeted them and grabbed an apple, then swung back out of the kitchen munching as she went. She quickly changed out of her work clothes and into her jeans and left the house, grabbing a second apple as she went. June's thin lips tightened, 'It's not right,' she began.

'What love?'

'A young girl only seventeen, coming and going as she pleases, it's not right. She could be up to anything.' Sid took another mouthful. 'Sid, I'm speaking to you, oh no, don't speak with your mouth full I beg you,' June said, touching the corners of her mouth with her napkin. 'Here, use your serviette not the back of your hand, if you wouldn't mind,' June suppressed an enormous sigh and inserted a tiny morsel of food into her mouth, carefully avoiding any interference with her lipstick. 'I mean, Sylvia could be having an affair for all we know. Pass the cruet, dear,' June said, grimacing slightly as Sid forked chips into his mouth.

'Well, we are, why shouldn't she?' said Sid, a little taken aback at voicing an opinion.

'She's *horrible*!!' Sylvia said to Michael. They were lying under the spreading branches of a copper beech tree on a perfect summer evening. 'She's always on about putting a 'doily' under the 'gateau' and using the best china for important guests. It's all 'serviette' and 'cruet' and she says she's going to get one of those *horrible* dogs with hair all over its eyes that looks like it hasn't got any legs and it's going to cost £50!!! That's more than I take home for a week's work!'

'I'd like to meet this monster.' said Michael laughing.

'You wouldn't. She'd think you just fell out of a tree with a banana in your hand wearing a bone through your nose and a grass skirt. She says all black people, 'coloureds', she says, should be sent home. There's no point arguing with her, she only gets worse.'

'Does she call us jungle bunnies and chocolate drops as well?' Michael laughed again.

'It's not funny, Michael,' Sylvia was frowning but Michael laughed. He rolled over towards her and kissed her. Sylvia loved the way he kissed, very softly and tenderly, kisses like talking without words.

Michael got home about midnight and hung his jacket on a hook in the hallway. At first he didn't notice Elizabeth at the end of the hallway, her arms folded, her face grim. 'What happened to you?' he said smiling. The smile died as she said, 'Who is she? A white girl we heard.'

'You heard?'

'People talk, they seen you in the park, other places too. Michael, white girls mean trouble. Mum and Dad are worried, they got nothing against white people, but it means trouble, you *know* that!'

'Elizabeth, it's up to me who I go out with black, white, big, fat, thin, boss-eyed, pigeon-toed. It's *my* business.'

'Don't say I didn't warn you.' Her stern expression faded and she pulled her brother's hair. 'I got nothing against white people either, it's just I got something against trouble.' She smiled and kissed Michael's cheek. 'You lovestruck idiot!'

'You'll like Sylvia, Elizabeth, you really will, but when you meet her you've got to be nice, not all fierce and feisty. She's sort of shy.' Michael went into soft focus thinking about Sylvia, and Elizabeth laughed.

June was teetering along, the dog under one arm, a white handbag over the other. She always shopped in the area on the other side of the borough, which she said was 'nicer', complaining that there were 'hooligans' in the local shopping street. But that day she couldn't be bothered. The dog wriggled and June put it down beside a tree. 'There you are Awnjelleek,' she wittered, 'does baby want a poo poo?' June glanced round, treating herself to the enjoyment of storing up details of the area to punish Sid with later: filth on the street, too many people, too many 'Pakis and coloureds'. As two women in saris came along the pavement, she took a very deep, very unnecessary breath and made as if to shelter her dog. 'Good little baby,' she said as the dog whined to be picked up again. As she lifted it up, June glanced over the road.

'And there she was in broad daylight, brazen as you like, with a coloured boy, holding hands. I hid behind a tree and watched her, and they *kissed*,' said June shuddering. 'Your daughter kissed one of them.' June glared at Sid. 'The sooner we get out of this area the better.'

Sid was perplexed. He'd never thought about anything particularly, didn't much care what political party was in power or whether a person was black or white. 'Oh,' he said.

'This is preposterous!' June said, chucking in a couple of big words, adding weight to her statements. Preposterous, extraordinary, utterly appalling were words she resorted to for emphasis. 'You sit there while your daughter is out with a . . . a . . . a nigger!' Her voice had risen several notes.

Sid stared miserably at the back page of the newspaper lying on the table, wondering for the first time if the impending marriage was such a good idea. Something was stirring inside him. To his surprise, and even more to June's, he expressed something of the feelings inside him. 'She's had little enough love in her life, you can't blame her.'

'Sid! But one of them! Just think she might be having sex with him.'

Sid made a supreme effort to think, not something he generally did more than was absolutely necessary. Life was something that happened and he had no desire to change or move or worry. 'Sylvia's a good kid,' he said trying to retreat from June's livid scrutiny.

'I can't believe this. What are you? I thought I'd found myself a man, I'm beginning to wonder!'

Sid was beginning to wonder too. He hadn't worried about anything since his wife's death, he'd closed down his emotions. He let the last few months surface. It dawned on him that it was only June's insistence and his laziness that had made them get together. He'd never have made the moves. It had been nice to have someone cooking and caring for him, fussing over him, someone to go to bed with at night. She had seemed a nice sweet woman. Perhaps he'd never really got to know her. All he wanted was simple human love, if he wanted anything at all. He thought of Sylvia and it was almost painful to register a sudden fierce protective love for her.

The door opened softly and Sylvia crept in, trying to get up to her bedroom before June heard her. June appeared at the kitchen door with the dog yapping at her feet. 'Come in here, your father wishes to speak to you.'

Sylvia looked at June with renewed contempt but trailed into the kitchen. She had never been afraid of her father. 'What is it, Dad?' she said, standing at the door. June looked pointedly at Sid who fiddled miserably with the newspaper, wishing he could immerse himself in the sports pages rather than face these women.

'It's all right love, you go to bed.'

'It is not all right, it is most certainly not all right!' June said. 'She's got to be told a thing or two, oh yes, and if you, her own father, won't tell her, then I damn well will!' June was losing control. Sylvia's eyes narrowed as she looked at June. June stood up. 'Now then, my fine miss, I was out shopping today and I saw you, and who were you with? Perhaps you'd like to explain!' She looked at her father who continued to fiddle wretchedly. 'Well, come along, let's hear your explanation. Going out with boys is natural at your age, but going out with coloureds is not natural, it's appalling!' June shrilled.

Sylvia had concentrated on not answering back since June had lived in their house. She had held herself in check, relying on her opinion that June was beneath her contempt to help her keep her temper. But this was a declaration of war and Sylvia was ready. 'Dad, what's your part in this?'

'Love, I don't mind but June is, after all, a woman and knows . . .'

'June a woman? She's not a woman, she's a painted doll!' Sylvia was losing her temper fast. 'She's a thing. She just paints her nails and her lips and cheeks and plucks her eyebrows and shaves her legs and armpits and bleaches her hair and covers her body up with deodorants and perfumes and has conned you because you're the only nice guy she could find who didn't see through her. Under all that paint and perfume is a rotten bitch!'

'You little hussy!' June screamed.

'And you're not my mother, you're nothing to me, you've no right to tell me what to do. I make up my own mind and I love who I like. It's my business. I'll go out with black men if I want to, I'll go out with whoever I want to.'

'You'll do nothing of the sort! You'll stop in until your father has seen this boy's family and warned them off, and we'll be leaving the district as soon as possible. Too many Pakis and niggers for my liking and you'd bring one of them into the house given half the chance.'

Sylvia yelled at June, 'Just go away, I hate you!' June took a step closer, simultaneously raising an arm, and Sid watched as June's long vivid pink nails left a trail of colour in the air before they dug into Sylvia's cheek. Her other arm swung round and she clutched at Sylvia's hair. Sylvia cowered as June lashed and clawed, screaming obscenities.

Sid felt as though he had been deaf, blind and paralyzed for a very long time and suddenly his faculties returned as he dragged June away from his bleeding and distraught daughter. He shoved her out of the room saying, 'Pack now, go, leave us be' and he slammed the door on her. Sylvia leaned against the wall weeping. Her father shyly put his arms around her.

'Sylv, those scars have almost gone,' said Sid.

Sylvia was taking down the foaming net curtains and putting up the old plain ones. She had an idea. 'Dad, shall we burn these? And we could burn the hat for the toilet seat and the lace table mats!'

'Let's save the table mats, I rather like them, we'll burn the rest if you like.' They laughed. 'There's more, you know. What about that bedspread? The one with all the pink stuff and hearts stuck all over it?' He chuckled. 'Yes! Let's go and look round, we might have forgotten something.'

Father and daughter went upstairs like conspirators, and bit by bit took things off walls and windows, shelves and doors, piled them up in the backyard. They were about to put a match to it when the bell rang. Sylvia ran to the door. It was Michael. He kissed her and remarked on the bright- ness of her eyes. She disentangled herself from his arms; she'd seen something by the door. She tore at a wooden varnished sign which June had bought during her French phase, 'Chez Nous'.

Michael followed her through the house, asking what was going on. Sid was standing in the yard, matches in his hand, waiting excitedly for Sylvia. 'Hello, Michael, nice to see you,' he said. 'Ready Sylv? Oh, what's that? Chez Nous!!!' and as he flung the match onto the rubbish, Sid began to laugh and so did Michael and Sylvia.

Sweet Sisters

I wish my name was Gloria Devanney, but it isn't. My name is Lily McTaggart. I get teased. They call me Silly Lily and Taggy. I will call you, my diary, Gloria Devanney. Dear Gloria, Gloria, Gloria.

In my room there are posters of my favourite pop stars and also a ballerina and a picture of a little girl that is old-fashioned and she has a blue dress on and a puppy with a bow in its hair. I talk to them without opening my mouth because I am lonely. I had lots of friends when we were in London. This is a list of my friends in the order I like them best: Harriet Tennant, Sandra Howard, Tracey Berman, Shirley Parker, Nancy Mallinson, Joanna Gilmore, Wendy Parker.

Wendy Parker's last now, although she used to be my best friend. She told a teacher I forced her to eat a toffee which had been in my mouth which wasn't true. Susan Green isn't even on the list because on Tess's last birthday, when we were in London, my dad who knows a keeper at the zoo got them to bring a pony to our street and everyone got rides. But that weekend Susan Green invited me to her house and I wanted to go because it was very nice to go away by myself. I made up my mind and missed Tess's party. But in the morning when we woke up, Susan Green said 'Does your tooth hurt where they took it out' and I said 'Yes'. She said 'Aren't you going to cry and

173

I said 'No'. She came over and punched me in the face and I cried. She laughed and said I looked funny crying and called me 'Silly Lily', so I ran down the stairs and I rang up my mum. It was only 7 o'clock Susan's mother said. She had pink hair. I asked my mum to come and get me. She did and I missed Tess's brilliant party. I hate Susan Green.

Now we're in the country and there aren't any kids except one called Mark. He says hello. He carries a stick or a pitchfork. I don't like him.

My mum and dad got divorced. I don't know why. They said they were getting a divorce. They stood very still when they told us. Tess ran away crying. I got under the table. Dad took his bags and went away. He married this woman called Sarah. Mum married this man called Steven. Me and Tess came here to live with Mum and Steven.

I don't like Steven. He has a fat red face and laughs at his own jokes. Then he wipes his face with a red spotty hanky. He said I was silly because I was scared when bats flew into my room in the dark. I don't like the country. There are no cinemas. I roller-skate in the living room because it is huge. Mum says it was a ballroom. We only have furniture in two rooms, the kitchen and Steven's study. Mum says we'll have more one day and we all have beds. The house is very very big. Me and Tess went to the top floor. There were lots of rooms with nothing in them and the windows closed and hundreds of dead flies. And I saw a ghost. Steven says there are little brown ladies in old houses in Dorset. Dorset is where we are. It was a little brown lady that I saw. I wasn't scared but I didn't like to go near the cellar after that. The bats were worse.

The vicar had a tea party and me and Tess went. He made all the kids play Racing Demon with ten packs of cards on the grass. It was raining. Tess and I stole some

Craft Cheese Slices and ate them in a cornfield, the corn came over our ears so nobody could see us. I've done a drawing of a lady in an apron. She's thin and her little girl is crying. She says 'I've hurt my knee' and the lady says 'Oh my poor darling! I will take you back to the hospital.'

When Dad came to see us, he brought me this book. He said it was from Frieda. I am not going to tell him I write to you and call you Gloria. I miss Frieda. She lived with us in London. She looked after me and Tess. One day we were coming home from school, me and Frieda; Tess wasn't there. We got off the number 113 bus. Frieda held my hand because I was little. I said 'Can I have an ice cream' and she said 'No'. I asked why, because she always got me an ice cream. She said 'Because I haven't got any money.' I was surprised because grown ups always have money. I asked 'When will you get some more' and she said 'When your daddy pays me.' I asked 'How much does my daddy pay you' and she said '£17.50.' That's a lot of money but not for a grown-up. They spend that at the shops in one go. When we got home I stole 50p from Mum's purse and crept up to Frieda's room. She slept in the attic. I liked that room best in our house in London. She was asleep and I watched her; it was a funny the way her throat went up and down, and I thought how nice she is and I hoped she wouldn't die. I put the 50p on her table. Nobody ever said anything. When Mum and Dad got divorced she had to go home to Germany and look after her mother. I was very sad.

Dear Gloria. Dad took us out. We went in his new car. He said 'Let's see if it goes 100 miles an hour. Don't tell your mother.' We went up the motorway; it was very exciting I sat in front and pressed the radio buttons like it was an aeroplane and I was a pilot. I drew him a picture of a girl lying on her back wearing her brother's boxing gloves. Her very shocked mother is at the door. I don't know why I did it because I don't have any brothers.

I had a good game of nurses with a girl called Ingeborg Finkbeiner who comes from Germany; she came for a day with her parents. She said the patient should die. I wrote on a piece of paper that I will die when I am twenty on May 13th. Yesterday was Tess's birthday. She was eleven. I am nine. I gave her a box of coloured pencils and we went to see a film in a town where there is a cinema. Tess likes romance. It was this very very old film called *Romeo and Juliet*. Me and Tess cried a lot. Steven didn't come; he has two baths a day, and he's a writer. He sits all day in his study and writes in pencil. It digs into the paper underneath. He can't drive which is funny for a man, also he doesn't go to work like my dad does. When we lived with my dad we only saw him for five minutes at night and at weekends. It's August 3rd, it's ten to three and fifty seconds, fifty-one seconds, fifty-two seconds.

Dear Gloria. Dad came to see us again, and he said there isn't any such thing as God. His car has a squashy roof. You press a button and it goes up, but it gets stuck and he has to fold it down. Mum says there's no such thing as hate. I wanted to wash my hair by myself, but she said I wasn't old enough, and then she said I was rude. She left me alone and I got soap in my eyes and cried. When we lived in London our grandmother lived with us. But she died. The house was all packed up and Frieda went away. That's why I'm lonely. Also there is no street to play in, and me and Tess never used to play together because I liked the street and the kids, but she didn't. But today I walked behind Mark when he brought the cows home and he swung a stick and said 'Hup cows, hup cows', and then I said it too.

Dear Gloria. Mum and Steven got married today. Uncle Luke and Aunt Brenda came, and Sammy and Johnny, my little cousins. I love them. In London I used to go to their house on my own after school and play with them. They came for the day and Mum and Steven got married and now they've gone. I'm crying, but nobody knows.

I have written a play called *The Guests*. It is about a young man who meets an actress outside a bathroom in a hotel. He likes her but she has a husband, He says Isn't the tea cosy a chaperone? I saw that word in a book, it means someone that stops the man from kissing the woman. He says, 'It's very peculiar.' She has a pet leopard. He says he wished he was her pet leopard. He's lonely. He is surprised that she is married and he says to her, 'You didn't tell me you had a husband. You told me you had a swimming pool, a car and a chauffeur, and the leopard. This is a terrible blow for me!!'

Dear Gloria. I'm sorry it's so long since I wrote to you and now I'm ten. Mum has taken us to this school and it's not the same as at home when I can just write when I want to. I have to keep you hidden because the kids are pretty tough. They would tease me if they read it. Some girls have five-year diaries with locks and they hide the keys. It's a boarding school. Mum brought us here. We said goodbye and watched her drive away. Me and Tess stood at the end of the driveway. We were by ourselves. Tess stood close to me trying not to cry. I stared at these little ponies with big heads nearly touching the grass. Mum will come to see us in a few weeks.

Dear Gloria. We were very unhappy at first me and Tess. We were homesick. Now I like it because I've got loads of friends and there's roller-skating and you can climb the trees. But the punishments are awful. They make you stand in the corner at mealtimes in front of everyone, and if you won't eat your food they make you stay all afternoon in the dining hall until you've eaten it. I put it down my sleeves and in my pockets and then down the loo. Tess is still very unhappy.

Mr Crisp, the Maths teacher, is very stormy. He has black hair and jagged eyebrows like black lightning. I can't do Maths and he kept me behind and made my cry, but he cracks jokes now. If you're clever, you can get more than four sweets at breaktime. Everyone tries. If you get caught he takes them away.

There is a lady who is the headmistress she is very very old. Her hair is white and wiry, and when she laughs her face creases up like a piece of old cloth. She is very kind but she is strict and tough and teases you. She laughs and it frightens me because she looks like she will crack and fall into lots of pieces. Sometimes you go riding before breakfast but Tess doesn't like riding.

Dear Gloria. It's summer holidays now and we're back with Mum and Steven. Tess was right. Mum is pregnant. Tess and me have got these ponies for the summer that someone couldn't look after. We ride them and they are in the field behind our house. We are in a different house now. It's not as big as the other one and there is furniture in all the rooms. I'm eleven and Tess is nearly thirteen. Tess can't catch the ponies. They are called Rum and Brandy. I caught them both today, and Tess said it was her turn to ride Rum. Rum moves and Brandy doesn't. You have to flap your legs every step to keep Brandy going but Rum kicks and bites. Rum is very frisky. I said Tess couldn't have Rum because I caught him. She grabbed Rum and got onto him and trotted away up the side of the field which is very steep. I ran along the slope twirling a rope over my head and yelling. Tess isn't a good rider so she fell off and tumbled down the slope. She called out to me 'You've killed me!' and I thought she was fooling around but then she fell backwards and I ran to the house looking for someone. I couldn't find anyone. So I ran to the cottages up the hill. Mrs Wright came to the door and I begged her to come quickly. I said Tess was dying. I pulled her by the hand. She's very old, and she was puffing. She said 'Lily you'll kill me too!' and I was terrified in case they both died. Tess was sitting up waiting for someone to come, and when she saw us she lay right back down again. I saw her but Mrs Wright didn't. I didn't want Mrs Wright to say I'd got her out for nothing. And I was still scared.

I don't want Mum or Dad or Tess to die. I don't tell Tess I'm lonely because if anyone knew they'd think I was pathetic. Me and Tess fight so much they say we'll have to go to separate schools. When they say that we make up. Mum says we love each other really. Tess looks after me at school and on journeys from Mum to Dad.

Dear Gloria. It's still holidays and now we're in London with Dad and Sarah. It's not like in the country, but it's not like it was. They're in a street where there's nobody playing, no kids. Dad goes to work and Sarah has to look after us. It's more normal here than at Mum and Steven's. Tess and me go to museums and films in the afternoon with Sarah and to the shops. I miss Mum. And Frieda. Next week we're going to Italy.

In Italy, Gloria, I've got sixty mosquito bites. Sarah says the one with the most bites can have a box of chocolates. I sleep with my arms outside the sheets so that I'll get the most bites but I don't tell any of them because I want them to feel sorry for me. There's a dog I play with in the garden. Sarah's daughter Juliet is seventeen. She plays the piano and paints. She's very pretty and I'm scared of her. I am very ugly. It's very hot.

Dear Gloria. Back in England with Mum. We got the train back to Mum's. I didn't want them to know I was crying, so I said I'd go and look at the rabbits and ponies. I sat in the barn and cried because I missed Dad. When I'm with Mum I miss Dad, when I'm with Dad I miss Mum. When I'm at school I have to be tough so nobody will know I miss anyone.

Mum had her baby. He's called Peter. He's fat with red cheeks and he has a nanny. Nanny cracked a joke; she said 'What did the bra say to the top hat?' She told me to say, 'And what *did* the bra say to the top hat?' 'You go on ahead and I'll give these two a lift,' she said. I was shocked but I liked her better after that. I have my supper with Nanny. We watch TV and she says 'Oh that's nice, we'll have one of those,' when the adverts come up, then she laughs and winks at me.

Last night I heard Steven shouting at Mum so I went downstairs. He was drunk and staring at Mum. He told her to go back to London and called her awful names. I said I'd beat him up if he didn't leave my mum alone and he looked at me, his eyes all kind of stuck and gluey. Mum said to go back to bed.

Dear Gloria. They put me in this new school now I'm 13. I wanted to go to Tess's school but we fight so they wouldn't let me. It's very strict, and I'm not allowed home at weekends. You have two different uniforms every day and three kinds of shoes and you're only meant to be friends with the girls in your form in your house where you live. That's eleven girls. I don't like any of them. Two girls got caught in an airing cupboard, they were kissing. One was a vicar's daughter with red hair, and the other was called Ellen and she was quiet. They expelled them. They said they were lesbians. I asked Caroline Sawyer's mother – we were in her car and it was half term – why two cows in a field were climbing onto each other's backs. She said they were lesbians. Caroline Sawyer and her sister Rosemary laughed because I said 'No they're not, they're Jersey cows.' Mark had taught me all about cows. Nobody said anything so I thought lesbians were a kind of cow. I asked this girl Paulette who knew about things like that, and she said lesbians were girls that preferred girls, and she said they were disgusting. I didn't think they were. I knew the two girls and they were normal like everyone else. Everyone has pashes on older girls but if you talk to them they aren't friendly. I've got a pash on this girl Suzy Wilson. She talks to me when nobody is looking. She told me she was in bed one morning, and when she woke up there was a rook sitting on the bars at the end of her bed. I like her because she says things like that.

Dear Gloria. It's holidays again and I'm not going back to that school. They've sort of expelled me because they say I don't fit in. I rode a bike down the main corridor and met a boy called Phillip Melville and we smoked cigarettes and held hands. Also I drew a picture of a naked woman in green and pink pencil and the house-mistress Miss Wall said it showed I had a dirty imagination but I wanted it to be like the drawings Tess does at her school. They do life class and pose for each other in the nude. They made me stay in nearly every weekend and learn Shakespeare speeches. Miss Wall shut me in this little room. I tried very hard. At four o'clock she would get me out and tell me to recite them. She had little eyes with all baggy bits round them like the turkeys in the farm near the big house we lived in that summer. She made me do the one about Till Birnam Wood be come to Dunsinane but I could never remember it. It means I didn't see Mum for weeks. I'm staying with my godmother Jenny. Jenny is bossy but I like her. I heard her telling her husband one night, while I was sitting on the stairs because I couldn't sleep and I was crying, that Steven was trying to prove Mum was mad so he could get the baby off her. Jenny said he drinks. She said he rang up the school and told them Mum was mad so I shouldn't go home for weekends. Jenny said she thought that's why I got all those punishments at weekends. But she said 'Lily is very naughty,' Tess isn't naughty. I'm going to her school next term.

Dear Gloria. I'm at Tess's school now. We still have fights. I'm fourteen and she's sixteen. But she sticks up for me because I'm always in trouble. One night I pretended to go mad for a dare. I sat in a corner tugging at this little piece of paper for two hours. I couldn't stop. My best friend Annie wouldn't talk to me; she got the matron. The matron went to Tess. She said 'Tess, Lily has gone completely haywire this time.' I was in the sick room and I was crying because I thought I'd gone mad. Tess was allowed to stay with me that night, and she put her arm round me and couldn't stop giggling. They gave me hot chocolate and talked in quiet voices. Tess says Mum has left Steven now because he threw a suitcase at her head. I feel sorry for Mum because when you're forty you're supposed to be married.

Dear Gloria. Me and Tess and Mum and our little brother Peter are living in this house Mum got in London. It's falling down a bit. Mum types at night and when Peter is at school. She goes out at night sometimes, but she doesn't tell us where. Sometimes we meet her dates and I hope she'll marry one of them. I wish I had a boyfriend. I've never had one. I expect it's because I'm so ugly. I don't tell anyone I feel this way because I'm ashamed. I make out I'm OK and laugh a lot.

I'm going to be fifteen soon and Tess will be seventeen. She is going away to art school and I will feel very lonely without her. Tess is pretty now like Juliet. I'm not. I'm fat and I've got spots. My hair is too thick and straight. Tess has lovely hair and she's never had spots. She's slim and wears mini-skirts. I walk sideways because on this Egyptian vase Dad's got they are always sideways, and I think I look thinner like that. I don't eat but then I get lonely and have a biscuit and a cup of hot chocolate. Once you've had one biscuit you may as well have another until the whole packet has gone. But I'm not even hungry and then I hate myself and feel worse, but I'd never tell anyone. If anyone comes at meal times I hardly eat anything so they'll think I'm feminine. Mum doesn't know. I play the piano a lot. Mum says I should practice because I make the same mistakes every time.

Dear Gloria. I knew the headmistress knew I'd broken a lot of the rules. Everyone had been covering up for me. When I got caught coming in early on a Monday morning, I said I'd been writing poetry in the woods and in the cellar. They said 'Show us the poetry, and I did. It's real rubbish, but they think it shows I'm creative. I went with Tim in his old car for the weekend. We went to the sea and slept in the car. It was cold. He is just my friend, but they'd never believe that. Tess said I should watch it or I'd get expelled again. I told the headmistress I'd make a deal. I said 'If I tell you everything I've done, will you please not tell my mother because she's unhappy enough as it is?' She said 'All right.' I told her everything. She got paler and her lips got tighter.

Dear Gloria. I'm in the train. I've been expelled. I'm very unhappy and angry. I rang Dad and said 'Hello,' and he said 'You're coming home today.' I said 'WHAT?!!' and he said he was meeting me off a train at four thirty. I went into the headmistress's room; she had the parents with her of a girl that might go to the school. I called her a traitor. The parents looked very shocked. I called her other things. She said to them, 'I'm sorry but his girl comes from a broken home.' Then she let them out and went on her knees to me and said she had no choice but to expel me.

Dear Gloria. Mum was really glad to see me. She said 'Oh Good, you're home and we can have lots of fun!' I'll be sixteen in three weeks. I think I should stop writing to you because if anyone found out, what would they think. But I've been talking to you for so long. And nobody knows. Not even Tess or Annie. Tess has come home because she's not very well. The doctor says it's to do with her blood.

Tess is very ill, but nobody will tell me what it is. I'm not going to say Dear Gloria any more; I'll just write. I went to the hospital to see Tess. We were on our own. I showed her these pictures of when we were little, and they made her laugh: pictures of us with our hair parted on one side with hair grips, wearing frocks with smocking; of us in white sun hats with buckets and spades; of me holding a cat that looks as if it must have died shortly after the picture was taken, because I'm holding it by the neck; Tess picking raspberries, her cheeks the same colour as the raspberries. But then we started arguing. We often do. I said we shouldn't argue when she's ill. She insisted we finish the argument, and when I left she said 'Don't take it so personally,' and I said I didn't. I said I took it seriously. We argue about important things like war and God. Time keeps slipping by faster and faster. Tess is getting very thin.

Everyone said Tess would be OK soon and not to worry. It was Easter and I went to stay at Jenny's. I got back today and I went to see Tess. She's in a room by herself. The door was open, and I walked along the corridor. She didn't hear me because I had soft shoes on. I hardly recognized her. She had her back to the door and her lovely, long, chestnut hair was in a thick plait down her back. But she was so thin that for a second I didn't think it could be her. She told the nurse in a very slow voice that she wanted me to do her hair for her. I was frightened of hurting her because she is so fragile. We always laughed as much as we argued, but she hasn't got much energy so she smiles.

Dad came and he tried to make Tess eat. He gave her

strawberries one by one, and she very slowly tried to eat them. He was trying not to cry. Nothing has ever hurt that much. The way she ate reminded me of watching a tortoise when I was little; its eyes were half closed and its jaws moved very slowly as it took a tiny shred of lettuce. I don't know why I thought of that tortoise. Tess tries to talk to all of us.

I never got on with Tess's boyfriend Simon. I bumped into him in the car park outside the hospital. I said hello and he smiled. It was windy and my hair was in my eyes. He smiled very very sadly and kindly. He said 'Lily, Tess really is very ill.' I said, 'What do you mean?' He said that she might die. I felt very cold and we hugged each other.

Today was the first time for years that Mum and Dad were together. It was in a room in the hospital. They went into a garden just outside and were both pulling weeds out of a tub. I watched them. Simon and Juliet and I sat together in the room. We knew Tess was dying. Juliet sat very close to me. Juliet and I went in to see Tess. She held our hands and looked very slowly from one to the other of us and she said 'My two sweet sisters.' She never spoke to either of us again.

Dad took Mum home. Juliet and Simon and I waited in the hospital to take Tess's things away. I didn't want Tess to be alone. I went back into the room. There were three people in there. There was a man in a white medical jacket sitting on the end of the bed while two nurses put things into a bin liner and called out what they were. Tess was lying on the bed, a pillow under her chin. I was horrified and backed out. Soon after, the man in the white medical coat came and he apologized. Then a nurse with very freckled arms came to get me; she said if I wanted to see my sister again she'd come with me if I liked. She took me along the bright corridor and opened the door. The light was soft, the blind was down. I stayed with Tess for a while looking at her sleeping. I thought, 'she is sleeping.'